Praise for Lauren Dane's
Lost in You

"Readers will want to climb in between the covers of this story and never come out again. [...] Outstanding!"

~ *RT Book Reviews*

"Lauren Dane rocked this story like the pro that she is. As usual, she made me fall in love with her wonderful characters. [...] A very touching and romantic story."

~ *Long and Short Reviews*

"Wholly engrossing with everything I love in a contemporary romance, I think I will find myself reaching for this book again and again for a reread."

~ *Fresh Fiction*

Look for these titles by
Lauren Dane

Now Available:

Lost in You

Lauren Dane

SAMHAIN PUBLISHING

Samhain Publishing, Ltd.
11821 Mason Montgomery Road, 4B
Cincinnati, OH 45249
www.samhainpublishing.com

Lost in You
Copyright © 2013 by Lauren Dane
Print ISBN: 978-1-61921-493-4
Digital ISBN: 978-1-61921-285-5

Editing by Anne Scott
Cover by Kendra Egert

First Samhain Publishing, Ltd. electronic publication: March 2013
First Samhain Publishing, Ltd. print publication: September 2013

Dedication

Family is a gift. This one is for the family of my heart as well as the one of my blood.

Chapter One

What he needed to do was take a ride. He'd been dealing with his father, the move, getting all the stuff in place for the shop, and none of it was fun. Joe was tired of everything. He took a glance over to where Buck had sacked out, his face near his bowl should anyone try to take it. The dog snuffled his annoyance when Joe bent to stroke over his head but groaned a little when he got his ears scratched.

"I'll be back in a while. Don't sleep too much."

Buck opened one eye and then closed it again on a sigh. The sound of Joe's keys would have sent his normally high-energy dog jumping. But he'd been playing with the dog next door while Joe had been painting earlier and had taken several runs with Joe to the shop and out to his parents' place and clearly had had enough.

Joe got that. He wished he could lie near his bowl with a bottle of beer and sack out for hours too.

Joe snorted as he stood, looking out his kitchen window over Main Street. He'd finally finished unpacking the last boxes earlier that morning, and while he wasn't totally moved in, he'd already come home.

Petal had been part of Joe Harris for his entire life. Even when he'd been halfway across the world, he'd never been too far from Petal's streets. So when he backed the motorcycle out of the garage and started it up, he knew exactly where he wanted to ride.

It was a warm day. Sunny and clear, and once he'd gotten a little out of the main part of town, the scent of grass and trees replaced everything else. The hum of the road beneath him soothed nearly as much as the full-throated growl of the bike. He might have turned his life around, but a guy still had to have some fun. The bike was part of that fun. He'd miss his every-Sunday group he had back in Dallas, but he had so much to do now that he'd moved back home he wasn't sure when he'd be able to find a new group. But he would eventually.

He needed to remind himself of that. Right now things seemed overwhelming, but they'd mellow. He'd find a routine. Get his dad some help. Get his business up and running. Maybe even find some time to date around, or at the very least have sex.

For now, the road had to be enough.

For now, it was.

"You missed a spot."

Beth sent a look to her brother William. "Volunteer labor is notoriously imperfect. It's a sad fact of life." She rinsed off the window she'd been washing on his truck.

"You want to borrow the truck, you gotta wash it. That's the deal."

"I did wash it." She turned the hose on him, and he jumped with a hoot, sending kids hurtling into the yard, giggling and soaked. "And now I washed the owner. You want I should break out the soap and get behind your ears?"

He grinned and shook his head. "I'll get even for that."

"One day maybe. But for today, I am queen." She tossed the cloth back into the bucket and bent to turn the hose off, pausing to squirt the kids again.

"Thanks for the truck wash. And for watching the kids last night." Her brother winked before he looked over the yard. His kids were out there running through the sprinkler along with several of her nieces and nephews belonging to their other siblings. She'd had them all at her apartment the night before for a sleepover so their parents could have a date night. She loved each and every one of those munchkins, and it was a lot of fun to have been able to spend so much time with them.

Still, when she left William's she planned to go back to her place and take a long nap.

"No big. We made cookies and had popcorn and watched *Mary Poppins* a few times over."

"We still pretending you watched that one for the kids?"

"Plenty of sprockets young enough that I can keep that up a while longer." She grinned. *Mary Poppins* was one of her favorite movies of all time. She hadn't ever seen it as a kid. Her parents weren't much for Disney movies for their kids. That and they never had a VCR or anything like that. She'd discovered it when William's oldest had come along. By that point, years later, she'd seen it so many times it'd become a running joke in the family and she didn't care.

There was something fine and lovely about Mary Poppins with her perfect voice and quest for happiness in whatever task set before her. Plus, dancing penguins.

A low-throated growl of a motor sounded before she caught sight of the motorcycle that pulled up at the curb out front.

William raised his hand to wave, smiling.

"Who is that?"

"Joe Harris," William called back over his shoulder.

Holy sweet baby Jesus.

Beth stood still, unable to move or tear her gaze away from Joe as he swung his leg over the bike to stand. And that was before he took his helmet off and all that golden hair spilled out. Her parts came to life as she swallowed hard, taking in the bulging biceps, straining against the soft-looking blue T-shirt. Tattoos made her wonder if he had any hidden out of sight. Powerful thighs filled out faded and worn jeans. His boots were more work boots than cowboy boots, but they worked too.

Worked, much like the sunglasses hiding eyes she remembered were green. He looked dangerous. And hot. More hot than scary. Definitely hot.

He was the exciting older bad boy her brother used to run around with. In other words, total teenage-girl fantasy fodder.

"Hey, Joe Harris, what brings you here today?" William approached his friend and Beth had to rush to catch up.

She was glad she did because Joe smiled at William, showing perfect white teeth.

"Needed to get out for a ride. Thought I'd stop by when I came back through town to say hey."

He looked to Beth and she licked her lips nervously. And that was before he slid his sunglasses down, exposing those intense eyes as he took her in.

"Welcome back to Petal, Joe." She managed to talk to him like she'd talk to anyone else. Mainly because she was trying to pretend she wasn't imagining him naked and bringing her cake.

Ha. She was *totally* imagining him naked bringing her cake.

"Beth?" She didn't miss the way his gaze lingered on her breasts where her shirt clung. It wasn't white so she missed giving off the wet T-shirt thing. And good, 'cause kids and all, and because she didn't do wet T-shirt contests. But she was glad he found them nice enough to look at a while.

"Yep."

He got that look. The one guys got when they liked what they saw. Then his gaze darted to William, and the look changed to *oh yeah, that's my friend's little sister.* Damn. She was clearly going to have to knock him out of that box.

"Nice to see you. Last time I did you were still in high school, I think."

She was sure he never even noticed her as a person back then. "Probably."

He really looked good. Like, really, really.

But before she could get warmed up enough to flirt, he turned his attention back to her brother and she hid her frown.

"Come on in. I'm planning on some time on the porch. Gotta keep an eye on all these sprouts." William had pretty much forgotten about her now that his friend had arrived. *Boys.*

"I'm gonna run. I have an appointment in a while with my bed and a nap." She tiptoed up and hugged her brother, who kissed her forehead when she stepped back.

"Thanks again for watching the kids."

"Anytime." She looked to Joe again. "See you around town, Joe." And she totally would. Because now it would be her mission.

The kids all came running, laughing and squealing to give her hugs and kisses, and she told them she'd see them the next day at her sister Tate's house.

She didn't even try to pretend she didn't throw some sway into her walk when she headed to her car.

Chapter Two

Beth looked through her closet, trying to decide what exactly to wear that day. Since Joe had been in town two weeks—and because she'd failed to bump into him all those times she'd tried to—it was time to just go right over and say hello.

It was neighborly after all. Really, as a Southern woman it was her duty.

"Wear something red. Red is a great color on you. It's a confident color." Her best friend Lily riffled through her clothes and pulled out a dress she hadn't worn in ages. "This."

It was simple enough. Hit her right above the knee. A boatneck collar, which always suited her face. Sleeveless, which was good because it was August in Georgia and she didn't want to look any more sweaty than she had to when she stopped by Joe's garage to deliver her welcome basket of goodies.

And checked him out a little closer.

"I can't believe I missed it when he came over to William's place." Lily shook her head.

"You did miss an eyeful. When he rode up on that motorcycle, I nearly choked on my tongue." Beth bent, looking for the right shoes. Heels were sexy, but she was on her feet a lot at work so she needed low ones. "I suppose someone could say that was a welcome back." She frowned a moment.

Lily snorted. "That wasn't a welcome back. You were at your brother's house when he came over. Not the same. He's a friend of the family and back in town. You'd still take him something because that's what you do. If he's gay, married or otherwise unobtainable, then you say hey welcome back and go to work. No harm no foul."

"Thank you for enabling me." She winked.

"It's my sacred duty as your best friend to enable you." Lily smoothed over Beth's hair. "You have such gorgeous hair. Have Tate do something to it. A bun, some braided thingy, whatever. Then he can see your neck. You have a great neck."

Beth ran a hand down the front of the dress, looking at herself critically. "He'd probably rather look at my boobs. Boys like those."

"I wouldn't know anything about that. God, you're such a floozy."

They both dissolved into laughter.

"I've got to run in a minute. I brought the invitation to the wedding so don't forget to take it. Nathan is totally on to us both. He gave me that look of his when I was getting ready to come over here earlier."

"He's good at that look. Learned it from Tate, who is the master. But none of those boys is the boss of me so he'll have to suck it up. Still, he'll be a good daddy some day." Beth looked herself over in the mirror. She'd come a long way from that girl who had to make do with hand-me-downs and whatever Tate could find for them at garage sales and thrift stores. She'd made something out of herself. She was a business owner. She had a nice apartment. Her fridge and pantry had food, and the last time she hid from a drunken argument was years before, the last time she'd gone to her parents' place.

Beth Murphy had grown up and left all that crap firmly in

her past.

"You look so cute in that dress."

"Nice call."

Lily winked. "Always eager to help you snag a man. Since you're so homely and all."

"It's a cross I have to bear. Can't complain. I could be as ugly as you."

Lily rolled her eyes. "Ha. Okay, gotta go. I'm meeting with the principal in a while to talk about what's going on at home for Chris this school year."

Lily was raising her teenage brother, Chris, who'd had a pretty difficult time after his parents had split and their mother had descended into substance abuse. But Lily had made a huge difference in the boy's life and that surly kid who was likely to drop out of school was now back on track.

"Okay. Talk to you later?"

"I'll call you this afternoon or maybe I'll come by so I can hear about what happens with Joe."

Lily hugged her and was gone. Beth took one last look, dabbed her lipstick and grabbed the giant basket of treats her older sister Tate had baked, tucked the invitation inside and headed off as well.

Tate looked up as Beth stopped by the shop.

"I just wanted to drop off my junk and have you do my hair before I take the basket over. You have time?"

Her oldest sister smiled and motioned for Beth to sit. "You know how much I love it when you let me do your hair."

This was true. Tate had brushed her hair so much when

they were growing up that Beth often considered it like a hug or a snuggle with her sister.

She met Tate's gaze in the mirror. "Up you think?"

Tate brushed it out and thought. "Hm. How about braided away from your face here, but loose in the back? You have gorgeous hair so you should use it."

"Whatever you say. You're the artist."

"If only you were this easygoing about everything."

"If I was I'd be boring."

Tate made a little *hmpf* sound that always made Beth want to laugh, but she fell under the spell of having someone brush, pin and curl to get her all prettified.

Tate worked quickly and efficiently, braiding, twisting and securing. "So you know, William is going to break something internal when he finds out you've set your cap for Joe. Joe's reputation is less than stellar."

"Thank God no one judges what you were like at eighteen when it's over ten years later and your life has changed." She arched a brow at her sister, who just snorted and kept working.

Growing up in a household like theirs had conditioned them in some negative ways. But they were ways Beth was more than aware of. While she appreciated Tate's concern, Beth wasn't their mother.

"Look, if he's like Dad, I'll walk away. You know that. I like 'em bad, with a soft, gooey filling. I don't want a lazy drunken lout who'll knock me around when he gets bored. And he came back to help out his family. Jerks don't do that. You know his parents don't have any money or anything he'd be after. William says Joe's changed a lot since he left Petal. I'm going to see for myself."

Tate nodded, but said nothing further for a while until she

stepped back, giving Beth's hair a quick spray.

"Damn you're pretty. Pulling your hair back only highlights that."

Beth smoothed a hand over her hair with a smile. Another fucked-up thing from their childhood. Tate was clearly not their father's child, a product of one of their mother's multiple affairs. And their father had never let Tate forget it. He'd spent decades trying to crush Tate into nothing. He'd used the fact that she was short to her siblings' tall, curvy to their lean, blonde to their brunette to try to hurt her. Not that their mother did a thing to stop it. But Tate had never let it break her, and she'd never made her siblings feel bad about it either.

Probably helped that Tate had herself a man so gorgeous he could walk into any magazine ad selling cologne in a heartbeat. And that the man practically worshipped her and their babies.

"Hopefully it'll work."

"If he can resist you in that red dress looking the way you do *and* carrying a big basket of cookies and brownies, he's not worthy. He might even be kind of slow. Which, you know, given the way he lived all those years ago, he might be."

Beth laughed then. He'd been quite the partier in those days.

"He sure looked like he was living better. Damn. He's..." Beth fanned her face. "He's ridiculous, that's what he is. Tall. At least six and a half feet tall. And muscles too."

Tate waggled her brows. "Hurry on up then and get over there. I want a complete recap when you're finished."

Beth took a deep breath, grabbed the basket and headed out. His auto-repair shop was only a few blocks down, and there was no time like the present.

Joe Harris had just about finished with the carburetor he'd been working on most of the morning when he heard the click of footsteps and came out to see who it was.

The jingle of Buck's collar alerted Joe he wasn't the only one attracted by the sound. He grinned down at his dog before glancing back toward the doorway.

He froze at the sight. Beth Murphy looking better than a body had a right to. He'd thought she'd been pretty amazing the first time he'd seen her a few weekends back. She'd worn cut-off shorts and a T-shirt then, but this Beth was gussied up in a pretty red dress, her hair shiny and reaching nearly to her waist.

He wondered what it would feel like against his bare skin and then mentally slapped himself.

"Hi, Joe!" She thrust a giant basket at him. "I just wanted to stop in and welcome you back to Petal. Officially I mean." She shrugged and smiled prettily.

He took the basket and put it on the counter. "Beth Murphy, look at you, girl."

She looked down at herself and back to him, a sparkle in her eye that he liked immensely.

"I'd give you a hug but—" She indicated his overalls, covered with grease and dust from crawling around under the truck he'd been working on.

"Sorry. Been a busy morning."

Buck barked a few times, not a man to take being ignored lightly and she knelt. "Why hello there. Aren't you handsome? I'm Beth. Who are you?"

Buck barked again, dancing around her, his tongue lolling as he checked her out. She laughed, scratching behind his ears.

"That's Buck. Don't get on her dress."

Buck gave Joe a look that told him the dog had no intention of being on the outs with the woman.

"Did you come to work with him to keep him out of trouble?"

Buck barked again a few times, and laughing, Beth gave him one last scratch and stood. "Sounds like that's exactly what he's doing."

"He likes to keep me company. I found him at a garage so he's at home in one."

"Someone abandoned him?"

Joe liked the outrage on her face.

"He was so tiny. I found him in the dumpster out back. Someone had thrown him away like trash. I wasn't sure if he'd make it." Hell, Joe had bottle-fed him for a while until he got stronger.

"Honestly! Some people aren't fit to breathe air."

Buck barked again and then plopped down, his head on her shoes. He gave a one-eyed glance Joe's way, as if to tell him not to let her go. Joe would have to explain the meaning of best friend's little sister to Buck later.

"Well you did the right thing and he looks like he's got a good home now." She leaned close and he caught her scent. Jasmine. On another woman it might have been too much, but on her it was rich and sensual.

She held up a cream envelope with his name on it. "This is an invitation to Nathan's wedding. Lily—you might remember her though she's a little younger—anyway Lily wanted me to drop this off for you while I was here."

She had a lilt to her voice. A drawl that also seemed sort of breathless as she delivered her words at top speed. Joe had no idea how she managed both at once, but she did.

"William said he was engaged. Figured Nathan would never settle. He sure did love the ladies."

She laughed. "He still does, but Lily's all the lady he can handle. They're good together." She paused and that smile crept back over her mouth and his heart skipped a beat.

"You're worrying me with that smile."

It brightened, and he became fascinated with how glossy her bottom lip was. Plump and juicy. He wanted to lean in and lick over it.

"You're awfully big and brawny to be askeerd of a girl like me."

He laughed. It'd been a long time since he'd teased back and forth with a woman and it had felt this natural. "You forget I grew up around you Murphys. A girl like you is exactly who I'm scared of." That and her big brothers.

She took his hand and squeezed. "So, Joe Harris, you should take me to lunch so we can catch up."

"Should I now? What if I brought my lunch?"

"But you didn't. The Sands is delightfully air conditioned and they have lunch specials. And pie. I may be able to sweeten that deal with some gossip. I'll even let you pretend you don't care about that sort of thing."

How could he turn down pie and air conditioning? She was his friend's sister after all. No need to be unfriendly after she'd come over to welcome him back so nicely. And Buck was going back home for the afternoon anyway because it was too damned hot in the shop.

"All right then. William sort of caught me up on all the Murphy stuff, but he's a man of few words. I imagine you have more to say than he does, and you'll give me all the information about who is up to what."

She smiled again. "Good. I'm at the salon right up there." She pointed. "Tate, Anne and I own it. Come by and collect me when you're ready." She turned and headed to the garage door before pausing and looking back over her shoulder. "Don't make me wait too long, I get grumpy when I'm hungry."

With a wave she was gone, but he sure as hell watched that delightful sway as she moved across the street and then to her salon.

"So I think Thunderbirds are go." Beth gave double thumbs-up as she moved to her desk. Anne and Tate did most of the hair work while Beth did the books. She did the occasional shampoo if she was needed, ran errands, handled supply orders and pretty much everything else.

The sisters were all so close, so used to having to work together, that it was smooth and efficient when others may have had a struggle.

"Do tell." Tate stood behind her client as she spoke.

"Delivered the goods. A man'd have to be blind to overlook a basket full of your baked goods."

"And your boobs." Anne grinned up from where she'd been mixing some color.

"Well, yes. I did wonder if it was too much a gamble to go with a dress that didn't show any cleavage."

"He has an imagination. They're right there under the material, after all. Men are pretty good at remembering where your boobs are."

Beth grinned at Tate. "Yeah. Good point. Anyway, I pretty much cornered him into going to lunch with me today."

"Nicely played. He's coming here to pick you up?"

"Yes."

"Good. We can get a look." Anne rubbed her hands together, making Beth laugh.

"Don't scare him away."

"He grew up surrounded by Murphys. There's no hiding from that. Anyway, he's got his own scary reputation to overcome. He'd best be a good guy or you know how many Murphy older brothers are going to come down hard on him." Tate raised one brow as she kept working.

"It's lunch. We're not getting married, for crissake." She waggled her brows.

She was still grinning when the bell over the door jingled and she looked up to find him there. He'd gotten rid of the coveralls and stood in jeans and a T-shirt with those sunglasses on.

"This place is crawling with Murphys." He looked around, smiling.

"We're notoriously hard to get rid of." Beth grabbed her bag and headed to the door. "You remember Tate and Anne? Girls, of course we remember Joe." She looked up at him. "We've been gossiping about you for two hours now."

He blushed. "I'm not sure how to take that."

"Good." She looked over her shoulder and told her sisters she was off to lunch and would return in an hour or so.

He opened her door, a very good sign.

"Tate looks pretty much exactly the way she did back in the day. Anne used to have brown hair like yours, didn't she?"

Currently Anne was rocking some auburn hair. "She did. Her specialty is color. You never know what color she'll come in with on any given day. I was thinking about that shade of red too."

He slowed down, frowning as he looked her over. "Don't. I mean, it looks nice on her. But your hair is..." He shook his head.

"Well go on then. Is what? Ugly? Gross? Fabulous?"

He barked a laugh. "I keep forgetting how you all are. It's pretty. I like all the gold in it. In the sun I mean. Brunette is underappreciated. But it works."

"Nice answer."

He opened the door for her at the Sands and they went in. Petal was a small town. Small enough that everyone looked up to see who was coming in. She waved to a few people.

Roni, the owner, waved back. "I'll be with you two in a bit. Grab some menus. That booth over there is empty."

She obeyed, pausing to peruse the pie selection, and she grinned when she saw the cake.

"Cake day. Score."

He slid in across from her. "What?"

"They have cake today. Coconut frosting. My favorite. Do you like cake?"

He paused. "I feel like this is a test."

"Well?"

"Pushy."

She laughed as she watched him. The light coming in the windows seemed to glint off his hair. "You have great hair."

"Um, thanks." He slid his fingers through it. "Yes. Yes I like cake. Don't know about the coconut part, though."

"Well, you're halfway there. The pie is awesome too. Have the peach. I have it under very good authority that it's really good."

"By good authority do you mean you had some?"

"Don't tell anyone, but I have a baked-goods problem. Really don't tell Tate, as she's like the queen of baked goods and I had some here instead of at her house. She's territorial."

"What'll you give me if I keep my mouth shut?"

She raised a brow and leaned in. At first he dug it and then got nervous. This was flirting, but they had chemistry. Like whoa.

She frowned. "Stop that."

"You're an incredibly random woman. Stop what?"

"Stop thinking of me as William's little sister. You weren't there for a bit. And then you remembered. How on Earth am I ever going to get you to kiss me if you keep that up?"

His laugh was a little uncomfortable, but he was saved when Roni came over to take their order.

Once they were alone again, he sighed and caught her gaze. "You *are* William's little sister."

"So what?"

"So it's a fact. You and I both know it. Let's talk about something else."

She let it go for the time being. She'd be back. She knew he was interested. Good thing she was patient. She'd been bored with the men in Petal for years. He was the best thing to come along in ages. She wanted him and that was that.

"So, tell me why you're back in Petal and I won't pester you about kisses. For a little while anyway."

"You promised to catch me up on all the doings around town. So you first."

She sniffed, but sipped her iced tea and shrugged. "Well, my sister Tate married Matt Chase and they have two kids. There's another one on the way too. You know William is married, of course. Tim is married as well. Lots of kids all over the place. Each is cuter than the last. It's a trial, I tell you, being an aunt to all that adorable."

"I take it you love kids."

"Well, other people's kids most especially. I can fill them up with sugar and pretend we're watching all the Disney movies for them. They provide excellent cover for my addiction to Doritos and *Mary Poppins*. Oh and cake. But if you tell anyone that I'll only deny it."

"Gotta admit I was surprised to hear about Tate marrying Matt Chase."

She narrowed her eyes at him. "And why is that?"

"Wow, I saw some scary shit in Iraq, but that face? Ranks up there. Why you mad?"

"Why you surprised? You don't think Tate's good enough?"

He laughed. "Yeah, because I'm so high falutin' and stuff. I'm from the same part of town you are. I meant she was in my class at school. Tate is younger and she never hung around in that crowd. It's not a matter of good enough. It's a matter of who you know. That's just reality." Though he liked how protective she was of Tate, he was sorry to see how defensive she was. He understood it. Once he'd been away from Petal and had come back, he'd seen the stark differences between sides of town here that he hadn't really had to contend with out in the rest of the world.

"I apologize. It's a hot button. Tate went through hell at first. The stuff people said to her. She's pretty much a mother to me. What happened to her when she should have been all about falling in love with her man, it makes me so mad."

He liked a person who could own it when they did wrong.

"It's okay. It's good you spoke up for her."

"The Chases have been so amazing. They've just sort of enfolded all of us Murphys into their family. Polly Chase treats William's and Tim's kids like grandchildren, like she does Tate and Matt's kids. Makes a difference when their biological grandmother is a drunken loser."

He took her hand to squeeze it briefly. "You have a fine family, just not that part."

"Okay so why are you back?"

"Family stuff. I've been gone for years, it was time for me to come back. My parents are getting older." No need to destroy a perfectly lovely lunch with any talk about his dad.

They ate until he remembered exactly why he'd missed this place. Fresh, great food. Neighbors all around who stopped from time to time to welcome him back to town. Beth helpfully told everyone that he'd taken over the Conway Auto Repair and needed the business. He wasn't proud, that was how you got yourself new customers. And he couldn't deny how much he liked watching her in action.

"You have a lot of energy." They walked back toward her salon and his shop.

"You'll turn my head with all your compliments, Joe Harris."

He laughed. "It's a compliment. I promise. You know everyone and everyone seems to like you. You have a way with people."

"Ha. Not all people. Some people I want to hit with a shovel."

"In my experience, Beth Murphy, some people need to be hit with a shovel. Do you need me to take care of any shovel

27

smacking on your behalf?"

They paused near the pretty, flower-lined walk leading to the door of the salon. "You'd hit someone in the face with a shovel for me? Wow, you totally dig me."

True. But he shouldn't.

"It's a service I offer to all little sisters of friends."

Before he realized it, she'd tiptoed up and given him a quick kiss on his lips. She stepped back, a smirk on those pretty lips. "I should warn you up front, I aim to demolish that line of defense."

"Now why would you go and do that?"

"Notice you're not arguing." She turned and walked away, waving over her shoulder. "See you later. Thanks for lunch. Oh and cake. But remember, mum's the word on that or Tate will do me bodily harm."

He stared at her, a stupid grin on his face, until she'd gone inside.

Chapter Three

Joe rolled over with a groan to answer his phone. Buck grunted from the foot of the bed where he was most assuredly not supposed to be sleeping. A quick look at the clock told him it was just after midnight.

"Hello?"

"I'm sorry to wake you."

It was his mother, worry in her voice. He sat, more alert at her tone. "What is it?"

"It's your dad. He got all worked up. I was getting rid of things. You know what the garage looks like. I'm afraid it's a fire hazard. He got angry and then he left."

"Did he hurt you?"

"No. No. He just, he left in his pajama bottoms. He's been gone two hours. I'm worried but I don't want to leave in case he comes back here."

Joe scrubbed his face with his free hand. "Okay. I'll get out and start looking as soon as I can. Hold tight."

He pulled on jeans and a shirt, stepped into his boots near the door and hurried out. He might have to deal with cops, so he was sure to run a comb through his hair before he grabbed his wallet. He'd take his truck in case he found his dad and needed to give him a ride home.

Buck followed along and waited with a bark for Joe to pick him up. "Lazy bones." Buck snorted and then licked Joe's face.

The deteriorating situation with his father's mental health is what bought him back to Petal at long last. His mother couldn't handle it on her own anymore. He had a sister, but she lived in Maine and had a family to take care of. Joe knew he had her support when and if he needed it, but it was his time to be there and get things done.

Petal was small enough that he'd be able to do a drive of the main part of town in about ten minutes. But his parents lived on the outskirts of town and the neighborhood—though it was better now than it had been twenty years ago—wasn't the best, so he wanted to start there and work his way outward.

After about half an hour, he spotted a man sitting on the swings at the park. Joe took a chance and pulled to the curb.

"Stay."

Buck gave an annoyed snuffle, but moved to the window facing the park, getting nose prints all over it.

As he came around the car, Joe knew the man was his father. It was a warm night so at least he didn't have to worry about the cool temps and his dad out there in his pajamas.

Carl looked up at Joe's approach, but there wasn't much to it. Blank and a little sad.

"Hey, Dad." Joe lifted a hand casually. He took up the swing on his dad's other side. "Want a ride home?"

His father used a bare toe to push himself back and forth just a little. His expression, when he finally looked to Joe, was confused. His heart ached for a moment.

A wave of helplessness washed through Joe. This was way more than he was equipped to handle. There was something so wrong here. How the fuck was he going to make this better?

His dad's eyes cleared a little, and he looked around and back to Joe. "Hey, Joseph. What are you doing out so late?"

"I could ask you the same." He tried to keep his tone upbeat. "I'm looking for you. Mom's worried. You've been gone for a while now. How about we go back and get her to make us some tea?"

His dad stood when he did, following along, a little lost. Growing up, Joe's dad had always seemed so big. But in his bare feet with his pajamas and his thinning hair in disarray, he felt smaller. A shell, and Joe had to swallow back all that emotion. He needed to focus, to get his dad home safely. Then he could deal with the rest.

"You'll have to share the front with Buck."

His dad grinned at the dog. "Spoilt."

Joe laughed. "So much."

Carl scratched the dog's ears as Buck rested his head on his thigh.

Joe didn't know what to say. Or to do. He felt like he should admonish his dad for running off the way he had. He could have been hurt. But one look at the confusion on his father's face and he knew it wouldn't be heard. Maybe not even understood.

He didn't know what to do about any of this stuff.

The drive back to his parents' place was quiet. The streets were pretty empty. Thank goodness for Buck, who seemed to calm his dad down just by being there.

He pulled up at the curb and they got out, Buck hopping down and trotting next to Joe. His mother opened the screen door and took his father in.

She looked...*old*. Joe realized his dad wasn't the only one who appeared smaller and more fragile. Coming back to Petal was more than taking them to the grocery store and watching over his dad's uneven moods. This was so much more.

"I was worried about you." She reached out, tentative, to touch his dad's arm.

"A man needs a walk every once in a while." His dad was gruff, but there was a lot of emotion there, just beneath the surface.

Standing there, unsure of what to do next, Joe noted the front entry was full of boxes and garbage bags.

"What's all this?" his father asked.

"Your stuff. I pulled it back in. I'll call first thing tomorrow and tell them not to come collect it." His mother must have been planning to donate it to the charity shop in town.

Carl looked at it, opened a few boxes. Junk. Christ, it was boxes of stuff Joe knew damned well his father hadn't used in years, or had more updated versions of.

His dad turned his attention to Joe. "Your blasted mother is throwing my life away."

Her mouth hardened. "I don't hardly think so, Carl. The shed is going to catch fire. Or rats. It's full to the rafters out there. You don't need any of this. Everything you use is in the garage. You know I didn't touch any of that stuff."

Joe noted how worn thin his mother appeared. He wished he knew how to help them both. But he didn't. This little moment between the two wasn't the issue. He understood enough to get that.

The problem was huge and he was one person.

One problem at a time. That was the one way he could see to get through this. He needed to draw on his training and simply deal with one thing. And then the next. And the next. It was the only strategy he could imagine that could solve what seemed pretty insurmountable.

"How about some tea? Maybe a little something sweet to go with it?"

His mother sent him a grateful look. "I think I can do that. Come on through. I've got some leftover roast beef for Buck. He should get a treat if everyone else does."

He had tea at the dinner table with his parents. His mother moved around the room, pretty much the same way she had his entire life. The tabletop was smooth from use, from plates moving across the surface for decades. It was comforting here. Even his father had calmed a great deal. The confusion he'd been wearing on his features had faded, easing the panic that had seized Joe's heart.

Buck was dozing in a far corner, on the cool linoleum, sprawled to get the full benefit on his belly.

They sat for a while in sort of companionable silence. Joe didn't quite know what to do next so he let his mother lead.

Finally she patted his hand. "You should get on home. I know you have to work in the morning."

He glanced her way, hoping she understood. Maybe he should sleep over? She gave him a slight shake of her head.

His dad had wandered off in the direction of their bedroom, which was at the back of the small house.

"Thank you," she said in a quiet voice as they headed toward the front door.

"How often does this happen?" They hadn't really had the frank conversation they needed to. She was uncomfortable, he knew, and truth was, so was he. But avoiding it any longer wasn't possible.

She licked her lips, her gaze skirting from his. "He just needs rest."

Joe combed fingers through his beard. Time to push a little, though he hated to. "How often?"

"Sometimes he wanders off. But he comes back."

He scrubbed hands over his face. "Like once a month? Once a week?"

"Used to be once every six months or so. More often lately. Like once every few weeks."

Cold dread settled in his gut. "Mom, he needs to see someone."

"He refuses. I tried to get him to the VA hospital in Atlanta, but he won't do it. He'll be all right. He just needs to settle. Relax a little."

Joe would do some poking around to see if they couldn't get someone out their way. Maybe a home visit. This couldn't go on without some sort of medical intervention.

"Mom, he can't just go running off into the night. That's not being tired. There's something wrong. This could be dementia, or something else. I don't know. But it's not going to go away. He could get lost. Or get hurt."

"Don't be silly. Who's going to hurt an old man? This is Petal."

"He was in the park. Alone. No shoes on. He didn't recognize me at first. Didn't know what he was doing out there."

"Well and he's home now, isn't he?" She shook her head. Denying with her body language that there was any problem. It broke his heart nearly as much as it frustrated him.

"Now that you're here, he'll be better. Go home."

He sighed as he and Buck headed to the truck and back to his place. Things were most assuredly not fine.

Beth carted a huge tray of hot dogs and slider-sized

hamburgers over to the table where the kids were sitting in Tate and Matt's big backyard. A loud celebratory chorus met her, and she laughed, kissing heads as she did.

Little hands grabbed the food as she squirted mustard and ketchup on things when asked to. Tate insisted on fruit salad instead of chips, but the kids thought that was just fine.

"I'm going to get y'all some extra napkins. Be back in a sec." She headed to the table near the barbecue to grab some and some juice boxes as well.

William loomed nearby, and when he saw her, he sidled over, pretending to be nonchalant in a way a guy who stood well over six feet tall could never be. She knew it was only a matter of time before her brothers approached her about Joe.

"Let me take these over and then you can ask me whatever it is," she told him before returning to the kids' table with the promised napkins and juice.

She grabbed her own burger and began to lay tomato, onion and pickle on it. "So?"

"Joe says you and he had lunch last week at the Sands."

"We did. It was nice. Cake day, dontcha know."

He sighed. "What's your plan here, Beth?"

"It is my plan to make sure there is bacon the next time we have burgers." She grabbed a root beer and cracked it open.

He sighed again and she took pity on him. "I'm feeling magnanimous so don't get used to this. Are you asking about me and Joe?"

His grimace made her smile. "Yes. He's...well he's older than you are."

"He's five years older than I am. Let's get to the heart of the issue. I like Joe. In a I-want-to-kiss-him sort of way. He of course is trying to hold on to the whole *you're my best friend's*

35

sister so I can't touch you in your no-no places thing."

William flinched. "God. So leave him alone then."

"Look here you." She turned and narrowed her eyes at him. "*I like Joe Harris.* He's a nice guy. I know he was a wild one when he was young. But you were too and now you're a family man. People can change. Also, I'm a big girl. Five years is nothing. Anyway, if he didn't like me, he wouldn't be so panicked. You and I both know it."

"It would be so nice if one of my sisters was unassuming and sweet."

She guffawed. "Wrong family for that. But I can handle him. Anyway, you're acting like I'm going to elope and have eleventy billion of his babies next week or something. We're at the *hey I like you-like you* stage still. That's the best part. Don't ruin it. You know I'm going to have him if I really want him. I'm totally good enough for him."

He shook his head and took her chin for a brief moment. "Honeybunch, that was never in question. You're beautiful and successful, and as far as your brothers are concerned, there's no one who's good enough for *you*. He's just, he's seen a lot."

"Yeah? Fancy that. I have too."

He shrugged. "I guess that's true. And I know you're strong enough to kick any man who'd hurt you to the curb, though you'd have to get in line. But he was in Iraq for four tours. He's seen a lot. I just don't want you hurt."

She grinned. Her brothers were all big, gruff men. But beneath the surface, they were each giant marshmallows for the women in their lives. It was a good thing. Made her lucky. "Thank you, William. I mean it. Thank you for looking out for me."

He sighed. "You're going to pursue him anyway, aren't you?"

"Duh. And there's already the fact that you and he are friends from way back. We know he'll fit in just fine."

"You'll at least keep me updated? Not on any details of a physical nature or I'll have to pound his face. But you know the general stuff?"

"I sure love you." She dodged his question neatly before she patted his arm and headed off to the table where her sisters sat.

Still, it was a week after that conversation with William, and Beth hadn't seen Joe around town for a few days. She'd waved his way when she'd walked past the garage some days prior, but he'd been talking with a customer and she'd been on her way back to the salon so there hadn't been time to stop.

So she clearly needed to take the next step and she said as much.

"Go get some, girl." Lily spoke from her place in the chair. Tate was going over a few different styles of wedding hair. The date was a ways off, but it was fun and it made them all happy.

Tate cocked her head as she held a curl up and then shook her head. "Too foofy."

"What's foofy?" Anne sat on the other side of Lily as they all chatted.

"You know, dumb. Lily's not a curls-up-near-her-face-in-a-fountain kind of girl."

"Thank God or we'd have to taunt her." Beth shrugged. "Back to me, hello. God, Lily, does everything have to be about you?" She winked and Lily laughed.

"Just go on down to that garage and lay some sugar on him."

"He's a giant. I'd have to pole vault to get him by surprise. I

37

need to corner him somewhere."

Tate glanced up, catching Beth's gaze in the mirror a moment. "Why not at the garage? Okay so we know he's too tall to surprise with a smooch, but you're a total pest. Really, no one I know is better at cornering someone. Go over and say hey. I brought cookies today anyway."

Beth grinned at Tate. "You did? Have I mentioned lately how much I love it that you're like my baking fairy godmother?"

"Of course there's cookies. I knew I could get rid of them somehow and this is for a very good cause. I like it when y'all are happy. And you want Joe so I'll do all I can to help. I even set some aside for Matt. He's coming with the babies to have lunch with me."

Tate and Matt had two gorgeous children and another on the way. Matt's mother, Polly Chase, worked with Matt, whose schedule changed at the fire station often, to deal with childcare so Tate could still work three days a week. Even on those three days, Polly or Matt would often show up with the kids and a lunch. Tate would brighten a thousand watts at the sight of them.

It thrilled Beth because no one she knew in the universe deserved that kind of happily ever after than Tate. And it made Beth ache for it herself.

She hugged her sister, kissing her cheek. She patted Lily's shoulder as her friend gave her a thumbs-up. "I expect a full report back on the status of the Joe situation."

"We all do," Anne added.

"Right!" Beth gave herself the once-over in the mirror, touched up her lipstick and then grabbed the cookies, heading to the garage to deliver them.

Beth wasn't surprised to see the other single women of Petal had noticed Joe. He was super hot in that bad-boy, works-with-his-hands, has-a-scruffy-beard way. In other words, her type.

The thing was, *she* wanted him. And so the Dollys and Steffies of the world needed to get that through their heads. Everyone in their family joked that Beth was the queen of stubborn.

Ha.

She was. Which meant all these other hoochies had to hit the damned road. She pulled her phone out and made a quick call.

Once that was done, Beth tossed her hair back and walked in, right past Dolly, who wore a questionably tight, extremely low-cut shirt as she thrust her knockers at Joe.

Buck saw her and barked, nearly skipping—cutest damned thing she ever saw, his little prancing dance—over. Joe sent a look her way, part pleased, part pleading to be freed from Dolly's clutches.

"Hey, Buck." She bent to scratch behind his floppy ear and straightened. "You ready, Joe?"

Joe blinked and then nodded. "Yes. Ready."

Beth put the cookies on the counter and turned to Dolly with a smile. "Hey, Dolly, thanks for keeping Joe company until it was time for him to take me to lunch."

"He never said anything to me." Dolly tried to look triumphant but she just looked dumb. As usual.

"Why would he?" Beth laughed and turned to Joe, who'd grabbed his keys. Lunch was impromptu, but she didn't want Buck here suffering, not that Joe would leave the dog there

39

anyway. "Want me to grab Buck's leash?"

Joe couldn't help but be impressed by Beth. She breezed in, looking amazing. Especially in comparison with Dolly who apparently didn't believe in the less-is-more philosophy.

The damned dog actually danced to her, barking happily. And she had cookies? He could totally take her to lunch just for that. Then she'd saved him from Dolly and made sure he understood she wanted Buck along?

Every time he ran into her, he had less and less defense against her charm. Because she *was* charming.

And really hot.

He handed the leash to Beth and turned back to Dolly, once again pushing the bill and the keys her way. "So like I said, I changed the oil and checked everything over." He'd known, of course, that there was not a damned thing wrong with the car and that Dolly had been interested in him, not his mechanical skills. But he remembered what she'd been like in school and that had left him sour on her ever since.

Beth bent, chatting to the dog as she got him leashed. "Sorry, the cookies are triple chocolate and dogs can't have chocolate. Which really sucks, Buck, because chocolate is awesome. But I promise to let you have some of my ham sandwich as a consolation prize."

Joe held back a smile, shaking his head, amused. Dolly gave an annoyed huff, but paid and stomped out.

"Every single woman in town is going to be bringing in dog treats now." Beth straightened, handing the leash to Joe.

"None of them mean it."

She shrugged one shoulder. "I still aim to make you go to lunch with me." Buck barked. "And you too, Mister Buck. I haven't forgotten the promise of the ham sandwich."

He opened the door, locking it in his wake after he put out the lunch sign. "I need to lock the garage. Hang on a sec."

He needed to hire someone else. Which was actually a good thing.

"There's a nice shaded picnic table behind the salon. We of course have a very lenient dog policy." She said this as she knelt to get eye to eye with the dog. He liked how she was with Buck. It wasn't fake at all. She was as goofy with Buck as she was with Joe.

"He's going to leave me for you at this point."

She grinned, standing. "We can get sandwiches and stuff at the Honey Bear. I called ahead so they'd be ready. I hope you don't mind."

"Ever since you mentioned food, I've been starving."

She handed him the leash again, and took his arm. He should have stopped her. But he didn't.

She indicated the table under a big oak tree as they walked past the salon. "It's the Murphy version of a break room."

He laughed and very nearly leaned in to kiss her temple. "Why don't you and Buck head over. I'll grab lunch and be back in a few."

"Fine. I'll get some water for him. To wash down the ham sandwich."

He walked a block down and then across the street to the Honey Bear bakery and café. William worked there, Joe knew, as a baker. The early hours and solitary nature of the job suited his friend well. Joe got that too. He liked his job. Liked solving problems with an engine on his own. Puzzling through and going step by step to finish.

No one got on his nerves. He had no boss to take orders from either. It was just him and the thing he was best at.

He recognized the woman at the counter, and she grinned, holding up two big bags. "Got your order ready."

"That's some kind of service. Thanks."

She wouldn't take his money though, saying that Beth was like family and they had a deal with the ladies at the salon. He shoved a ten in the tip jar and headed out.

But when he got back across the way, she was lying on a blanket with Buck, scratching his belly. The dog opened one eye as Joe approached.

"He likes to drink from the hose. I told him he could have it from the bowl, but he snorted at me and got dog snot and spit on my leg. We had a talk about such behavior, and he assures me he won't be repeating that again."

She got to her feet, joining him at the table where she'd laid out some paper plates and stuff. He thought he'd be cool, sitting across from her, but that only meant he saw her face fully. The way her hair lifted now and again on the breeze.

He unpacked the bags and found she'd ordered two large sandwiches and a potato salad for him.

"Lots of food here. Thanks." He tipped his head. He liked that she'd handled the order, that she'd figured he'd be so hungry. Though he wasn't a fan of the idea that they didn't let him pay.

"I figured you'd be hungry. Tim can put away like four sandwiches when he's been out on calls all morning. It's meatloaf-sandwich day." She shrugged as she unwrapped a plain ham sandwich on thick-cut white bread. "This is okay, right?" She meant giving it to Buck.

Joe laughed. "He's a garbage disposal. Considering what I routinely have to make him stop eating, a ham sandwich is a good deal."

She grinned, breaking it into a few pieces and handing them Buck's way. He groaned and then devoured the food.

"I like to pay my own way."

She looked up from her potato salad. "What?"

"They wouldn't let me pay. When I picked the food up."

"William has baked for them for nine years. We trade haircuts and the like for food." She shrugged. "You can pay me back with other services. If you like."

An image of just exactly what she could exchange with him burned through him like a fever.

"It's a small town, Joe. That's how things work. Have you been gone so long you forgot? These sandwiches aren't a handout."

The thing about Beth is that she had the ability to put him in his place without making him feel chastised. And, he realized, he'd pushed a button he hadn't meant to.

"I'm sorry if I made you feel that way. You've built something here with your sisters. Hell, so have William and Tim. Nathan. All of you Murphys have dug in and made something of yourselves. You did something nice and I was a jerk."

She sighed, absently petting Buck, who shot him a baleful look. "We've all got our issues. Apology accepted."

"I feel like an asshole."

"You can take me to dinner next time. Make it up to me."

"We've talked about this already."

"You've blathered on and on about how I'm William's sister, and I've already told you that doesn't matter. Not in the way you keep insisting it does." She studied him carefully and licked her bottom lip.

At his reaction, which was a startled sort of groan, she smiled. "You should know your resistance will only make your surrender all the sweeter."

Chapter Four

Nathan strolled right into her apartment like she didn't have a front door. "My, did we forget our manners?"

He put a six-pack on her counter and gave her a look. "You should lock it. You're a woman living alone."

"I just walked in from work about two minutes ago. My hands were full. But you're right. If for no other reason than to keep the riffraff out." She eyed him.

He sighed so she decided to poke at him for kicks.

"Do you need me to give you the talk? You know if you put your thingy in her she could get pregnant with your baby type people, right?"

He appeared horrified and then dissolved into laughter. "God, you're gross."

"Nathan, if you think it's gross to put your thingy in Lily, you probably need a whole 'nother kind of talk."

He punched her arm. "Quiet, you. I wanted to thank you."

She smiled up at him. "For what?"

"You've been really good to Lily. You know, with all the planning for the wedding and stuff. She's got a lot on her plate and her own family isn't much use."

"Sit. Crack one open." She knew he needed to vent about Lily's mother and that he'd never do it to Lily, who was already conflicted about the situation.

"You know me so well."

"And I love you anyway." She winked and poured some chips into a bowl, pushing it his way. He slid a beer hers and she clinked it against his. "What's she done now?"

"She's probably not going to come to the wedding. Lily is heartbroken, though you know she's trying to pretend she isn't."

Lily's mother had gone to rehab after her drinking and mental-health situation had gotten so bad she'd neglected her teenage son, and Lily had given up her life to come back to Petal to take care of things. Chris, her brother, was back on the straight and narrow once again, thriving in school. Lily's mother had opted to go from rehab to a sober living house that was nearly four hours away.

Beth took a deep breath, wanting to make him feel listened to, but also saying what needed being said. "She's going to be far better able to live her life when she does come home. That's the biggest thing she can do for Lily and Chris both." She took a sip of her beer. "That said? I think it's shitty she won't even come out for the wedding. It's one day. An important day for a woman who gave her whole life up to come back here to do her mother's job."

He grumbled. "It makes her sad. I hate that. I can't protect her from that kind of sadness."

Her brother had lost Lily a decade before by being a dumbass. Since she'd come back into his life and he'd won her over, he'd been very protective of her. She knew it hurt him as much seeing Lily hurt and not being able to help as it hurt Lily that her mother was MIA.

"She knows you love her. That's the important thing."

He rolled his eyes and she rapped his hand with a nearby

pen. "Don't you roll your eyes at me. Lily needs that love. She needs to know you're there for her. And you are. That means everything to her. Her mother? Well, look, Nathan, she could be a drunk like our father and never do a damned thing. Would you rather that? She's trying. In her own way, she's trying to get better and come home. The recovery process takes time. She's got a lot of shit to get over."

"What about the shit Lily has to shovel while she's gone?"

"She couldn't handle it. Right? That's just reality. She's trying. Which took a lot of guts. Give her credit. I know you hate it that it's left Lily with that burden. But in the end, her mother is trying to get herself together so that when she comes back, she can handle that burden again without breaking. She's got to be afraid, you know? She was a mess when she went to rehab. For a woman who had as much control as Lily's mom, facing that had to be a huge thing."

"Don't take her side." He frowned, but she knew he heard her. Knew she was right.

"I'm always on your side. You know that. I know you're upset. I know you want to protect Lily, and I'm all for it given how Lily is my best friend and all. And I know you came here so you didn't spill all this in Lily's way because she already feels enough angst, guilt and anger about it."

"You're pretty smart."

She shrugged. "We can't all be school teachers. But I get by."

"I hear you've set your cap for Joe Harris."

She groaned. "God, this town! What's it to you?"

"Oh ho! It's my sister sniffing around a guy with a questionable reputation, that's what it is to me. You don't need that kind of trouble. He's more man than you can handle, Beth."

She laughed then. "You don't know anything about me. Not that way. If you think I'd go after some jerk like Dad, you're out of your damned fool mind. He's not that way. He's a nice guy. He came back here to help his family out. He was in the army. He rescued a dog. Hardly the work of Satan's minion."

He tipped his bottle. "If you say so. You have good judgment. Mostly. But if he hurts you, I'm gonna kick the shit out of him."

She grinned, but refrained from mentioning that Joe was like four inches taller and a solid wall of muscle. It was the thought that counted. "You're so nice to me sometimes."

"I like to keep you guessing. What do you have to eat other than chips?"

"Nothing. I was just going to eat chips for dinner. Then I had hating-myself-for-eating-chips-for-dinner on the schedule after that."

"Girls. Come on. I'll take you to dinner. Lily and Chris may meet up with us in a bit. She took him to get shoes and shorts for gym class too."

"Why aren't you over at Tate's looking pitiful?"

He laughed as she grabbed her purse. "She's not feeling well. William and Cindy took the kids for a while. Matt is spoiling her for a few hours with a quiet house and the air conditioner blasting. That and I wanted a beer and a chat with my favorite little sister."

She grinned. "Nice one."

Her apartment wasn't too far from their favorite go-to Mexican place. More chips, giant margaritas, the best tacos ever and, as they entered, it was dark and heavenly cool.

"Thank God. I thought I was going to melt. My swamp cooler is ancient and it costs a million dollars to run."

"Days like this I think about my plan to get Lily to agree to buy a house of our own so we can have a pool. She doesn't want to do anything like that at her mom's place."

"It's her house anyway." Which was true. The house Lily grew up in was left to her in a trust. It had been a pretty cool thing because her father tried to pressure her mother into signing it over so he and his new and pregnant wife could sell it! Lily told them the news, told them to back off, and Beth had laughed and laughed.

"Yeah, and you know as well as I do, she'll never displace her mother."

Lily was a good-hearted person. She loved her family, and as much as Nathan was mad right then on her behalf, he wouldn't have loved her as much if she didn't have the same dedication to family as he did.

Lily's mother needed a home to return to. And so Lily would make sure that happened, no matter what.

The server led them to a rickety little table near the back windows and they sat. She didn't need a menu, but she did like what she saw coming in the door. She waved.

Joe Harris looked up, startled, and then smiled when he saw her and Nathan.

"Be nice or I will kick you in the goolies," she said under her breath to her brother.

"Hey. Nathan, it's good to see you. I wanted to thank you for the wedding invitation."

Nathan indicated the empty chair. "You should join us if you're not meeting anyone."

Joe sat. "Thanks."

Nathan nodded. "As for the invite? No problem. Just get us a good present."

Joe laughed, and Beth wanted to hug her brother tight for being so sweet.

"Hey, Beth."

She smiled, her belly filled with butterflies.

"Hey yourself, Joe."

Nathan grunted. "What are you up to? Back here in town I mean."

They paused long enough to order and then got back to talking.

"I took over the car-repair shop. I figure Polly Chase will keep me in business if no one else comes in."

Polly Chase was notorious for her horrible driving.

Joe kept on. "Everyone ends up back here. Funny, you leave thinking *thank God*! And then you miss it the whole time you're gone."

Joe Harris had a sweet side. Beth liked that.

Nathan nodded, agreeing. "I don't know that I got to that point for a few years. But by the time I was finishing up with my master's degree, I was ready to come back."

"I finished my BA a year ago. Took me a million years felt like. I don't know how you stuck it out through grad school."

Nathan looked up from his plate. "I don't know how you stuck it out through Iraq."

Joe's good humor disappeared for a brief time. He shrugged. "I nearly didn't."

Nathan made a sound and Beth knew he regretted his comment. "I'm sorry, man. I meant to joke. But some things aren't funny."

Joe waved it off. "If you don't laugh you cry, right?"

She wondered what the story was but didn't press. She had

the feeling it was bad. She knew it had been for so many of the soldiers who'd returned home. And for the families of those who hadn't.

"What did you do there? In the army I mean." She tried not to inhale her food and scare him off, but she was hungry.

"I was a mechanic. It was a good thing. I didn't think so at first." He laughed. "I didn't have any skills. Well, not any that would have given me a job instead of time in the state pen."

Nathan looked to her with a smirk.

"How long have you been back?"

"Two years. I knew I'd come to Petal eventually. I landed in Dallas a while. Worked in a friend's shop where I filled out my training with cars and trucks. Why did you decide to be a teacher?"

Beth watched as Nathan and Joe talked. Nathan was an interesting man with a big giant heart. He liked Joe. She could totally tell. It was more than the fact that they'd known each other when they were young. It made her feel more comfortable around Joe, and in the end, it would help her plan as well. Nathan was a good judge of character.

"The whole time we were coming up, there were times when I really just wanted to throw in the towel. Shit was bad at home. I didn't have the time for homework when we were trying to survive." Nathan ate for a while before he continued. "But those times when it wasn't Tate kicking my butt all the way to school, it was a teacher who reached out. Who cut me some slack, or who gave me a book that inspired me, who pushed me hard to do my best. I wanted to be that for other kids."

Beth loved that story. Nathan, for all his jokes and that gorgeous face, was a person who wanted to give back. It pleased her to no end that he was such a great role model and such a repudiation of the people who had given them life and abused and neglected them.

"All you Murphys have done well for yourselves. It's nice to come back home and see your friends living good lives."

"Tate wouldn't have allowed anything else." Their older sister was far more a mother to them than a sister. She'd taken the brunt of the abuse, had skipped a lot of school to clean houses and pick up side work to keep them fed. She made sure they all went to school, wouldn't have tolerated anything else. They had a strong family and Tate was at the heart.

"For a gal so tiny, she's pretty ferocious." Joe grinned.

"She totally is. And now that she's got babies? Even scarier. It's sort of awesome how people scurry out of her way when she's on a tear." Beth smiled, full of love at the thought of her sister. "I forgot to ask you the other day. How's your sister?"

"She's good. Lives in Maine with her husband and kids. He's an engineer. She works part time now that the kids are in school."

They chatted a while until Lily came in with Chris.

Beth had eaten her fill and stood to hug her friend. "I'm off. Take my chair. Hey, Chris."

Chris blushed bright red and waved.

"Let me walk you home and I'll come right back." Nathan stood.

"I'm perfectly capable of walking five blocks to my apartment. It's light outside. Also, it's Petal." Beth pushed him back into his chair.

Joe stood. "I'll give you a ride. I need to get home anyway. Buck gets lonely."

Nathan gave her a look and she rolled her eyes. A ride home from Joe was way better than hanging out with Nathan. She'd gotten her time in with her brother and that was great.

But her plan was getting Joe alone as much as she could. She hoped Nathan read in her features that if he messed this up she'd draw on his face with a permanent marker when he was sleeping.

Lily smiled all serene-like, reaching out to pat Nathan's hand. "I'm so glad you're still here, I'm starved."

Beth shot her a grateful look. "Appreciate the lift. At least I won't melt now." She bent to kiss Nathan's cheek. "Thanks for dinner."

"You coming to Tate's tomorrow?"

"As if I'd miss dinner at Tate's?" Her sister had a weekly dinner for their ever-growing family. All the Murphy siblings were there without fail, and quite often at least several of the Chases were there too. The yard was big, kids ran all over the place. A good time was had by all.

"Love you."

She grinned. "Love you too, goofus. See you three tomorrow night." She turned to Joe, who led the way out, his hand on the small of her back.

His truck was at the curb. "I was hoping for the bike."

"You like motorcycles?"

"I've never ridden on one."

He looked shocked. "Get out of town."

"I'm serious."

He opened her door, and she hopped up into the cab, waiting for him to come around the other side.

"Riding on a motorcycle is one of life's greatest pleasures, Beth."

"I'm on Maple. Just go up here and hang that first left." He followed her directions. "Then to 4th, go right and right again on Maple. So you should take me then."

"Huh?" He'd imagined taking her a few dozen different ways over the last few weeks. And then he realized she meant the motorcycle. "Oh for a ride?"

"Yes."

She smiled, and it made him all sweaty, both the good and bad kind. She was the wiliest female he'd ever met. And she was beautiful. And she had the most awesome boobs he'd beheld in several years.

"I'm the blue townhouse. The driveway on the right is mine."

He pulled up and turned the engine off, and she reached for the door handle.

"Don't you think about touching that door." He got out and moved around to her side to open the door for her. She hopped down.

"Look at you with your manners and everything. I should let you know, however, that I totally have opening doors down. It's a skill I've had mastered for many years now." She fluttered her lashes.

He snorted. "Look here, we may come from the crappy side of town, but I know how to open a lady's door. And I'm going to walk you inside too."

They walked to her front door and she unlocked it. He went in first and turned to leave, but she closed the door, backing against it.

She smiled that smile of hers, the one that made him sweaty.

"How about you and me make a deal?"

"I know I'm going to be sorry for asking, but I can't help myself. What deal would that be?"

"I was going to invite you to share a beer or two with me.

But Buck is at home all alone so we can't have that. So. Why don't you run home, grab Buck and come back over? Then you can enjoy a beer and Buck won't be lonely. Really, Joe, it's the neighborly thing to do. Otherwise you'd be rude. That would suck."

He couldn't help it, he laughed, he was so charmed. Damn it.

But. She was a temptation. A big one. He shouldn't have volunteered to drive her home in the first place, and yet, he'd jumped at the chance when he got it.

This was dangerous ground. But he had no energy to stop himself from going down a path that would end in kissing those damned lips of hers.

"You're fascinating to watch."

"Huh?"

She walked to where he stood. He told himself he didn't move because the hall was narrow and she was between him and the door.

She put a hand on his chest as she took him in. "Every emotion is all over your face. But I won't poke at you just now. A man can only take so much. Or so I'm told. Go get your dog. I'll be waiting for you." She stepped aside, and he sucked in a breath that was heavy with her scent.

He started to argue.

She rolled her eyes. "Really? You know you want to. So go on now. Buck will like the company."

He huffed a sigh. "Probably. He likes company. Beth, you know this can't be more than friends."

She raised a brow. "Oh good Lord. You're here in my house. Not because we're friends. You're going to run and grab your adorable dog to bring him back here, not because he likes company. You want to be with me. You want to get to know me not as William's sister. You're a grown-ass man. I don't play games. Life's too short."

He stared at her. She wore a short-sleeved dress with a collar that should have made her look matronly but instead only made her look better. More feminine. Her legs were long and sun-kissed.

Beth Murphy was flat-out beautiful. And she knew him from before.

"You know I'm bad news."

She snorted, one hand on her hip, an annoyed look on her face. "I know you *were* bad news. I'm inclined to cut a man some slack for what he was like at nineteen. God knows William had his problems when he was that age, and look at him now."

"You're very sure of yourself."

"I grew up in a household with a mother who threw herself at one man after the next because she has some gaping hole she can't fill. And no, I don't mean that to be a pun. I may have flaws, but I know my worth. I'm not desperate for a man who doesn't want me. If you didn't want me, you'd have left by now. Hell, you'd have said your goodbye at the restaurant and let Nathan bring me home. I'm too old and too tired to dance around what is totally clear. You're interested in me. In my lips, which you can't stop looking at no matter how many times you tell yourself I'm William's little sister."

She sighed. "Look, go get your dog and come back here. You want to. I know you want to. *You* know you want to. You don't have to marry me, for heaven's sake."

"I'll be back in a few minutes."

Chapter Five

"Buck, we're in trouble."

Buck looked up from where he'd been chewing on some rawhide. One of his ears flopped back as he barked.

"It's Beth. We're going to her house."

Buck hopped up, tongue lolling, big goofy grin on his face.

"Yeah, easy for you. But she's my best friend's little sister. A guy doesn't go there."

Buck sighed before he snorted and walked to the door, waiting, doing that little dance of his.

He would have spoken to Virginia about this in the past. But that wouldn't be so easy now. First, she lived in Dallas. Second, when they'd gone from friends to lovers the transition back had been rocky and pretty much impossible.

He'd tried to tell her it wouldn't work before they gave in and had sex. But he thought with his dick and she was an adult and they had some chemistry. But after a few weeks it had sputtered out and they'd never really been the same.

So he couldn't call her to talk about another woman. Especially when what he felt for Beth was far more than sexual curiosity. He wasn't that great at dealing with women, but he knew the one you broke up with doesn't want to hear about how a new one is something you'd never experienced before.

He could talk to his best guy friend. But that happened to be Beth's older brother. Not a good idea.

Buck barked again, scratching the door.

"Fine. But this is your fault."

He grabbed a bowl and some food, and they headed back over to Beth's.

She opened her door with a smile and then grinned to Buck. "Come on in."

Joe allowed himself to take a good look. Both at her, and her apartment. It was warm. Framed pictures all over the place. This was a woman who loved people and who was loved in return.

"Lots of pictures." He indicated her walls.

She nodded. "I like being surrounded by people who make me happy." Her living room had a sliding glass door leading to a small patch of grass. She had a table and a few chairs with a big umbrella out there.

"How long have you lived here?"

"Um, let's see. Three years now. I used to live in an apartment my landlord owns. I had my eye on this place a while." She shrugged. "When it opened up I grabbed it. Tate is forever on me about buying my own place."

"Roots are important."

She snorted. "Yes. For Tate, they're everything. Want a beer?"

He nodded.

"My yard is fenced if Buck wants to wander out and sniff stuff."

He watched as she bent to grab the beer from her fridge. His whole body hardened. Buck wandered over to see what she was up to. She spoke to him absently as she cracked the bottles open.

He held up a bag. "I brought ice cream sandwiches."

Her smile shot through him, pulling him closer.

"You did? I love ice cream sandwiches."

Buck barked. She frowned down at him. "Not for you, Buck. You'll get sick."

He snorted.

"He's a pig. You can't tell him no because he doesn't care. I brought his bowls but I'll keep him outside so he doesn't get food on your floor."

She laughed. "Do you feed him outside at your place?"

"No. But we have company manners."

She bent and pulled out a placemat. "I've got toddlers over here quite often. They're worse I bet. We'll put the bowls on this."

Once she'd fussed around and Buck had pigged out—and Joe and the dog both knew he'd just eaten at home—they settled in on her comfortable couch.

She clinked her bottle to his. "Cheers."

"Why'd you stay in Petal?" He'd asked it so suddenly it surprised them both. "I mean, you didn't have the best childhood here."

She shrugged. "I didn't. But Petal isn't about my parents."

No, but he'd noted the look in Dolly's eyes when she'd taken Beth in. The thing about travel, even to dangerous shitholes where people shot at him all day long, was that he could see where he came from more clearly. Petal was a good place in many ways. But divisions existed. Class mainly, though certainly race as well.

"At first? I stayed because I didn't have the means to go

anywhere else. I had an accounting job, and it was good enough to get me some healthcare and to pay rent. Tate and Anne started the salon, and they needed some more capital. I bought in. My brothers started having babies, and then I couldn't leave or how could I see those kids as often as I want to? Tate got married and had babies and she's...well, she's my touchstone. I could move a few towns over. I worked in Riverton a while before I came to the shop. But...I think I stayed as a big middle finger to the people who made fun of us because of our clothes and our parents. I'm still here because Petal is my home. Jill, my youngest sister, she lives in Atlanta. She's got a fancy life and a great job. But boy do I miss her. She's cut out for that life. Big and exciting. Fast paced. I like it here. I like the slower pace."

She'd been tearing the label off her beer and looked up, her gaze locking with his.

He wanted to kiss her really badly. Jesus.

He sucked a few gulps of his beer down and tried to break that moment, but she wasn't letting it go.

"You should take pity on me."

She smiled. "I should? How's that?"

"You should stop being so hard to resist."

She leaned forward, placing her beer on the low table. And then she climbed into his lap, settling in, her body facing his, the hottest part of her sliding over his cock.

"Am I then?"

Her hair slid across his forearms.

He couldn't find his words, so he nodded. This close he could see the freckles over the bridge of her nose, the gold flecks around her pupil. She smelled good. Soft and sweet. Sexy.

She wrapped her arms around his neck. "Resist me then," she whispered, her lips just shy of touching his.

He barely registered putting his bottle down. All he remembered later was the feel of her as he caressed up her arms. The warmth of her skin, the weight of her body in his lap as he shifted, his hands sliding into her hair to cup her neck, pulling her close.

And the electricity as the kiss began.

Her taste rolled through his system, taking over, filling him with a need so sharp he couldn't stop himself from rolling his hips, pulling her tighter against him. She moaned softly, tightening her grasp around his shoulders.

He swallowed that moan, taking it into himself right before he left her mouth, kissing across her cheek to her ear, tasting, nibbling. Her head tipped back, and he feasted there on the tender skin just below her ear. Her breath stuttered and he smiled against her throat.

Her fingers sifted through his hair, holding him in place. "You like what you like, don't you, darlin'?"

She laughed, straightening to dip and grab a kiss. "I do."

"You taste good." He nipped her bottom lip.

She leaned close, licking over his bottom lip. "Yeah? Ditto."

Beth couldn't believe she was finally in his lap, his arms around her, her lips swollen from his kisses.

And it was a million times hotter than she'd ever imagined.

He smelled so good it drove her nuts. Her skin was hypersensitive. Where his hand cradled her neck, the heat of him sent waves of sensation outward. He was big and powerful, and yet the way he held her, the way he touched her was totally controlled.

He settled into a kiss like he was on a long, slow Sunday

drive. He held her exactly how he wanted her. It sent a shiver through her.

Then he pulled her hair. Just enough to get her head back so he could kiss down to the hollow of her throat.

She was pretty sure she'd never been so turned on in her whole life and all her clothes were still on.

Her nails dug into the muscle of his shoulders as she writhed, grinding herself into him, needing more.

"Hold on there, darlin'."

The way he said darlin' made her all hot and needy. Hell, what he was packing inside his jeans made her needy too.

She managed to drag her eyelids up as he pulled her upright.

"Why am I holding on? We were getting somewhere good."

He laughed and she moved in for another kiss. Good God he tasted good. She squeezed her thighs to hold him in place, and he groaned, his hands sliding down to rest on her ass.

She moved hers to slide inside the hem of his T-shirt, his bare skin taut and hot, and man oh man she wanted him naked and in her bed. She'd have to keep him there for at least a day or two.

He hissed when she dragged her nails up his sides. "Slow down."

"What?"

He laughed. "You look like my nephew when his mom tells him he can only have one cookie."

"I want all your cookies, Joe Harris. I want to eat them all up."

His pupils seemed to nearly swallow the color of his eyes. "You're playing with fire."

"Thank God! I've been trying to get you alight for the last month. Have I not been totally blatant? Have sex with me!"

He laughed, and she found herself on her back on her couch, Joe looming over her. She wrapped her thighs around him just in case he wanted to do something stupid like escape.

"This is a dangerous road."

"That's why it feels so good."

He leaned down and kissed her again. Kissed her and kissed her more. Kissed her until she was slow, drunk on his lips and the feel of his weight pressing her into the cushions.

He was so intense. She'd never, ever in her whole life felt this on fire. On the verge of *something* she couldn't define. He was big and bad and totally masculine. It was the hottest thing ever. She burned for him.

He tore his mouth away from hers, chest heaving as he caught his breath. "I haven't even taken you on a date."

She grinned. "Did this just occur to you? Shouldn't you be thinking about, you know, other, better stuff?"

"We're moving too fast."

She heaved a sigh. Annoyed, she reached down between their bodies, grasping his cock through his jeans. He pressed into her hand and she squeezed enough to get his attention. "This doesn't think so."

"*That* is not the smartest part of me."

Beth couldn't help it. She started laughing. "Why are you so miserable? Jeez. Am I hideous? Does my breath taste like cilantro?"

Buck showed up, putting his face on the couch next to her face. "See, even your dog thinks I'm awesome."

"You *are* awesome. You're beautiful and you feel really, really good. And I'm an old guy with a bunch of jagged bullshit in my head, grease under my nails that I'll never get rid of and a bad reputation. And I want to fuck you so hard you have trouble sitting down for the following day."

A flush went through her at the rawness of his words. "Wow. My hand is on your cock. I am *not* pure and virginal. I am just fine with you fucking me so hard I need Epsom salts."

He sat up with a groan, and she couldn't take her gaze from his crotch for long moments. She wanted some of that.

"You deserve someone better. Someone who is gentle. Who doesn't look at you and want to rut."

"Oh for fuck's sake. Save me the bullshit."

His eyes widened.

"I'm not an idiot. I'm not innocent. I know what I want. I'm a grown-up. I want you. My God, I've been chasing you all over town for the last month. You can't lead me on like a...a clit tease! That's what you are. I demand you satisfy me sexually."

He groaned and then burst out laughing. "I am in such trouble."

"Not really. I mean, unless you have a punishment thing. I could probably work with that."

He blushed. "No! Not like that. You're really perverted. It's a good trait."

"So can we stop talking and get back to what we were doing?"

He pushed up from the couch and began to pace. She frowned at the sight. "I have a lot going on right now."

"Not as much as you could." She scratched Buck's ear.

"You're not helping."

"Should I be? Just say it. Are you with someone? Married? Engaged?"

"And if I was?"

"Then we'd have to be just friends. I don't fuck around with other people's men."

He paused and she felt sick. First that he was taken and she wanted him so bad. Then that he'd done all that with her and he had someone else.

"I'm not. Married or engaged, I mean."

She got up and stalked to him, poking his chest. "You're an asshole. You scared me. What is your deal? You want me. I know you do." She grabbed his cock again. "This stuff about me being too good and your friend's little sister is just dumb. You're a big boy." She paused, smiling even though she was annoyed. "A *really* big boy. And I'm an adult. You're not a virgin and neither am I."

"I'm sorry." He turned to her, pulling her closer. "My father...he's not well. I'm trying my best but I'm not...I don't have the time for anything deep. You're not a fuck 'em and walk away type of woman. And not because you're William's sister. I like you. But I can't give you anything. Not right now. I'm drowning in all the things I'm responsible for as it is."

He had to go and be vulnerable.

"Okay, how about this." She led him back to the couch and sat with him. She handed him his beer. "I don't want anything from you but what you want to give. Take from me what I'm offering. First that's friendship. You can talk to me if you like. Second, that's some action in a naked, sweaty type way. I don't need to be taken care of. I don't think you're a cad but if you're with me, you're not in anyone else's bed. I don't need you to sing me to sleep every night. I don't need a ring. I pay my own bills. I own a business and have a life. Being with me doesn't have to mean anything more than enjoying our time together."

"I tried the friends-with-benefits thing. It didn't end well."

She laughed. "Dude, I don't want a friends-with-benefits thing. You and me? If we get naked and horizontal? We're in a relationship. I'm not saying I want your ring. But the fuckbuddy thing never works. Well, for you all—meaning boys—it does. But I know my strengths. If you were out there banging other women, I'd be miserable. I don't need to be with you every minute of the day. You're busy. I'm busy. But when we're not busy with other people, we can hang out."

He gave her a look. "This is the weirdest conversation I've had in a long time."

"You're from the South and you'd say that? Pfft."

He laughed. "Okay. How about I take you out on a real date? Like to a movie or something first?"

She was in his lap again, Buck barking happily in the background. "Are you worried for your virtue?"

"I've never met anyone like you before."

She kissed him quickly. "Yeah. I'm one of a kind."

She was. Damn it. He never should have agreed to any of this. But it was a way he could have her. And he really wanted her.

"It's Friday night. Why don't we go to the Tonk and dance?"

"No. It'll be noisy and full of people I try to avoid on a daily basis."

He kissed her chin. "How about a bike ride then?"

Her frown changed. "Really?"

"Yeah. I haven't had much of a chance to ride lately. Because you're such a horny woman, I only had two sips of my beer. We'll go for a long ride. I'll put a blanket in the saddlebag and we can make out under the stars."

"You've got a deal."

Chapter Six

He wasn't sure why he wanted to do a date type thing instead of fucking her right then. It wasn't that he didn't want to. He wanted to get her naked so much his hands had shook.

Joe couldn't remember the last time he'd wanted something so much. Especially something so fine as Beth Murphy with her bawdy mouth and her wise eyes. She'd seen a thing or three. He knew it because they had come up together.

She'd had it worse at home. He'd been poor too, but she'd been...worse. Her house was a battleground. A sick trash heap of abandoned hope. Of the bottle, of fists and angry words. He didn't know the whole of it, the details. But he understood enough, even from the outside.

Joe carried around a lot of rage. So much that he choked on it every day. But she didn't appear to. And of the two of them, she deserved to far more.

William had darkness inside him. He and Joe had been close enough to have gotten into more than a few fights together to blow off steam. He still had it, Joe could see, at the edges, though he now had a family, which had clearly centered him.

Beth though, Joe wasn't sure how she'd managed, but there was no anger there. No darkness that he could see. She was irreverent. Funny. Smart, especially about people. And dogs. But the hardness her mother had, the anger of her father, seemed to be absent.

She was beautiful and special, and while he couldn't give her the sort of relationship she deserved, he could give her a little bit of time before he tore her clothes off.

Joe grabbed an extra helmet, and Buck gave him a look, but accepted the new rawhide chew after he'd come back inside. There was a doggie door and everything, but Buck had been with Beth, in her house where everything smelled good, and now he was going to be alone for a few hours while Joe took her out for a ride.

"Dude, I want to spend some time with her. She's never been on a motorcycle she said."

Buck snorted but settled in to chew, preparing for an evening of napping. He raised one brow as if to tell Joe not to mess it up.

"See you later. Don't let anyone burgle me."

She opened her door, smiling as she walked right up to him, put her arms around his neck and tiptoed up, pulling him down for a kiss. Then she walked past, to his bike. She circled it, and goddamn if it wasn't sexy the way she touched it here and there. Peered at it, clearly impressed.

"This is a seriously sexy motorcycle. I'm just sayin'."

He licked his lips and moved to her, grabbing the extra helmet, handing it over. "Yeah? Just wait til it's between your legs."

She let out a shuddery breath and he let the satisfaction steal over him. He liked affecting her that way. It shouldn't all be one sided.

"I'm looking forward to it."

He got on and she followed, allowing him to help.

She didn't need to hold on. He could have told her she could sit up and hold the seat. But when she snuggled close against his back, those thighs of hers to either side of his body, the hot notch of her pussy against his back, he said nothing.

Her arms slid around his waist and he leaned back a little. She pressed a kiss to his neck, and he smiled, pulling out and then slowly down her street, heading out of town.

She lost track of time. Aware only of the way his back felt against her body. Of the way his muscles tensed and bunched as they took a corner.

The night all around them was glorious. The twilight casting a pink-orange glow on the world.

He pulled down a long road out toward the lake and stopped but didn't get off. He reached back, giving her an arm to help her down. She was tall, but he made her feel small. Not helpless. She liked it even as it sort of kept her off balance.

"I used to come out here." He spread a blanket out, and she sat, looking out over the hillside sloping down to the water.

"You did?"

"Back in high school. When things got shitty, or when I just couldn't take it, I'd drive out here and sit for hours."

"So did the military help you?"

He settled next to her, leaning back on his elbows. The fading light cast shadows on his face.

"I joined because I was on a bender." He snorted.

"That was dumb."

He laughed. "Yes. But it was a good thing." He paused, and she made herself be patient, hoping he'd say more. "I signed up in a stupid, drunken macho haze. Oh I was going to go over to *Eye Rack* and kick some ass. Until I went to basic and it sucked. God. I had to be up when someone else told me to be. I went to sleep when someone else told me. I ate when someone else told me. I was no longer in control of any aspect of my life."

The stars began to blink up above them as she leaned back to get a better look. He tangled his fingers with hers and she smiled.

"Did you try to get out of it?"

"Fuck yeah. I was miserable. They didn't give a shit that I was tired. They didn't give a shit about any of my excuses. Or my lack of control. I got into a few fights and got my butt thrown into the brig. I was thinking if they threw me out I'd be done. I just didn't care.

"And then my C.O. came to see me and was like look, son, don't be a dumbass. You have an opportunity here. You can go back to your shitty little town until you finally go to prison. Or you can use this time and experience to get yourself some self-control. Some skills you can make a living with."

Beth wondered if his father had ever said anything like that to him. Hers never would have bothered. She didn't know much about Joe's dad. He'd done odd jobs around a back injury and lots of unemployment. He was big though, like Joe. His mother had worked in the cafeteria at the grade school for as long as Beth could remember.

"So I got out and got into a mechanic's training program. I had one more narrow miss with jail, and that was it."

"Then you got sent to Iraq."

He wasn't sure why he was pouring his story out this way. He hadn't ever really done it. But there was something about her. The steady presence beside him, her fingers in his. She was strong. Beth Murphy didn't need fixing. Or shielding. It was...nice to say it. To talk about himself there in the deepening darkness.

"I was still an asshole. Not as bad once I'd sobered up. But I thought Iraq would be one way. But when I got there it wasn't." He licked his lips. "The people I met were good people. They weren't my enemy. You know? They had lives and then this war erupted all around them. Everything was different for them."

"Like it was for you I wager."

"Yeah. And I didn't have to go out on patrols regularly like other people did. There was plenty of stuff to be fixed all the time. Every day. The sand and dust got into everything, fucked it up. And of course there was sabotage. And getting shot at."

She got very quiet and he appreciated it.

"I went to Iraq not so much thinking of it as *Eye Rack* like I did when I first signed up." He was ashamed of that now. "But I figured it was easy. You know? Who the enemy was. But it's not. And you're in a public market and someone who smiles at you is the person with the fucking bomb strapped to his chest. Or the old guy you're suspicious of is the one who risks everything to tell you about a bomb he saw getting planted." It had fucked with his head for a long time. Everything he thought was true had been challenged. He'd seen so much death. So much destruction. He felt for the people in Iraq. Felt for the soldiers.

Sometimes he still woke up with his hands shaking, sheets wet from his sweat. But he was alive and he had all his limbs, which was more than some of his friends could say. And he had come back with a skill.

"It sucked. I learned a lot. They kept me longer than I'd have stayed given any choice at all. But it's over and I have a skill I can use to pay my rent. That's something. I never thought it. Not when I was young. I figured I'd have some shitty job out at the mill. If I was lucky."

71

The night air hung with the scent of flowers, of warm earth and bark from the trees all around them.

"I'm glad you're back."

He smiled because she meant it. It was a tease, yes, but she was being honest and it was really, really nice to be wanted.

"How'd you end up owning a salon?"

"I don't remember much. Not before I was nine or so. Tate says it's probably because of...well of how things were at my house. But I never did well at school. I got by. To have done any less would have been hard on Tate, and God knows she had it hard enough. Nathan, well, he always saw college as a way out. A way up. I never saw myself going to college. But after high school I took some accounting classes at the community college. Mainly to pass time. I had a bunch of crappy secretarial jobs. Anyway, I found out I was good with numbers and math. I liked it. I liked making things balance. Numbers make sense. There's a right answer. So I got this job at a medical office in Riverton. I saved my money, thinking about buying a house. Anne and Tate bought the salon, and I helped with the books. Volunteering at first. Helping with the ordering and that sort of thing. The whole family worked on the building. Painting, new drywall, stuff that would have been really expensive to have paid for. They got in about six months and needed more capital to keep going. I proposed to come on as a third partner. I had my nest egg, and boy let me tell you, it took a week of constant arguing with Tate to get her to do it. But in the end I bought in."

"Looks successful. My mom gets her hair done there, she said."

Beth laughed. "She does. I don't know her very well. Tate does her hair. But she seems like a very nice lady. We do all right. I manage things. Tate and Anne are the talent, so to speak. We have a nail person who comes in a few days a week and two others who have stations for cuts and color. Tate did a special class on how to do facials and that stuff, so she does a spa day two days a month. Those are popular. I have a good life. I never dreamed of it when I was a kid, you know? But it's a good life. I work with my sisters every day. I see my family all the time. I can pay my bills. My car is in decent shape. I have no real debt. And now there's this super-hot guy who's come back to town and things seem to be moving in a good direction."

He sat up, hungry for her. "We should go back."

She yanked on his arm. "Why? There's no one out here but me and you."

He kissed her slow and deep. "What I want to do to you might be illegal in Georgia. We should do it behind a closed door."

She laughed. "Put that way..."

He stood, tugging her to her feet. But then he swayed, holding her to his body. Dancing to music she made just by existing. He was tall, but so was she. She fit him so well.

They danced for some time as the night closed in all around them. Until he tipped her chin up and fell into that mouth once again. Until need raced through him, beating at him.

He broke away, handing her a helmet.

Then his phone rang.

He groaned and looked at the screen. "I'm so sorry. I have to take this." He turned his back and answered his mother's call.

He'd had a terse, quiet conversation before turning back to her, telling her he had to go, dropping her off at her place and speeding off into the night.

She'd asked if she could help, but he shut her down with a

shake of his head. He'd gotten on his bike without another word and waited for her to climb up behind him. Even back at her place he'd been quiet, not going in with her, just waiting until she'd gotten her door unlocked before he'd pulled back out and roared away.

That sucked.

She'd slept horribly, and though it was her day off, she'd headed in to the shop to keep busy.

"You want to tell me what's up your butt?" Anne put a cup of coffee in front of Beth.

"Nothing's up my butt, Anne. That's exit only, thank you very much."

Anne snorted. "Well your sense of humor still exists. So what's wrong?"

Beth huffed a sigh. "Okay so last night I managed to finally get some forward movement with Joe. I mean we had this scorching-hot make-out session and it was edging toward sex and then—"

"Make out? Like you're in high school? Did you let him touch your boob over your bra but under your shirt?"

"Listen here, sister. Making out is totally underrated. Sure, sure, once you're older and you can have sex, kissing for forty-five minutes at a time flies out the window cause, duh, sex. But, making out with Joe Harris is hot. *Anyway*, so we have this talk and things are great and he takes me for a ride on his motorcycle and we laid on a blanket out under the stars and kissed some more and he's like hey I want to fuck you hard and I'm like hello, let's get on that. And then his phone rings, he takes me home without more than four words and he's gone."

"Who was it? On the phone I mean."

"I think it was his mom."

Anne's horrified look nearly made Beth choke on her coffee. "Ew. His mom?"

"Hush up. Jeez, weirdo. I think he's got trouble at home. You know his dad hasn't been well." Joe had alluded to health issues in his family being part of the reason he came back.

"I didn't tell you this yet, but I heard Jim Bodry down at the hardware store talking about Mr. Harris. Saying he got into a yelling match with Merle at the post office."

Beth frowned. "He used to drink a fair bit. But not like Dad drinks. I wonder if it's worse now. I just wish Joe would talk to me."

"Give him a chance at least. It's only been a day. See if he calls you today."

"I was thinking of calling him."

Anne snorted. "He needs to call you. You were nearly doing it and he ran off? I'm not sure there's a Miss Manners for that, but if there was, she'd say he broke off the sexing so it's his job to call and check in. Like if he broke a date."

Anne met her eyes. "Look. I know you like being in charge. But you got that far enough. You pushed your way into his life and obviously it worked. Although he's lucky to have you. He's a guy. A big burly guy like William. He's going to need to be in charge now. Also? Honey, he needs to do it. *You* deserve that. You can only chase so much and now it's his turn."

That's when Tate burst through the door with her sister-in-law, Maggie Chase and a passel of kids. Beth smiled at the sight. Standing to go scoop up some smooches.

"It's your day off." Tate gave her a long look. "Why are you here?"

"Just can't get enough of Anne's sunny disposition I guess. What's up this fine day?" Beth gave her attention to Maggie.

"Hey there."

"The house is awash with Chase men watching sports. Lordamighty."

Beth looked to Anne with a grin. "And that's a complaint?" Every one of the Chase brothers was better than the last to look at. Gorgeous, great manners, sexy, and head over heels in love with their wives.

Maggie laughed. "Go on over and look. Really, it's pretty stunning. But noisy. Polly has requested a house full of babies, those are her words. So Tate and I thought we'd take them over. But we wanted to stop by to invite you two to lunch with us."

"Oh, lunch with adults. Doesn't it sound amazing?" Tate sighed happily and Beth felt a million times better.

"Yes, it does."

"I've got one last cut in about fifteen minutes. It's a quick one. I'll be done by one. I can meet you guys." Anne stood, stretching.

"We've got to drop off all the kids and stuff. It'll be around one before we're ready anyway. We were thinking about Chinese food."

"Oooh! Riverton?"

"Yes." Tate smiled. China Dish had been a favorite for as long as Beth could remember. A big treat now and then as they'd earned some money and wanted to celebrate. It wasn't fancy by any stretch, but it had good memories, big tables and huge portions.

"Be back here at one then. We can carpool over."

Maggie and Tate left.

"I'm going to run home to change. I'll be back to help you close up." Beth gave Anne a hug. "Thank you for listening."

Anne waved it away. "Of course."

She had dinner later on that night at Tate's so she figured she'd put on a little makeup and change into something pretty. It was good to look nice. It'd pick up her spirits maybe.

And she was doubly glad she'd done it when she came out her front door to find Joe pulling up to the curb in his truck.

He got out and looked her up and down real slow. "Hey." He shoved his hands into his pockets and loped over. She was glad she had her sunglasses on so she could check him out all sneaky-like.

"Hey. Everything all right?"

He sighed heavily. "Yeah. I'm sorry. About last night I mean. It was a family emergency."

"You wanna talk about it?"

"God no." He shoved a hand through his hair. "You free? I mean, I know you're busy and all. I just thought—"

"I'm not. Not right now anyway. I'm having lunch with my sisters. You want to come to dinner with me tonight? At Tate's? They're setting up a screen in the backyard and watching a movie after we eat. It's pretty fun. William will be there too."

He hesitated, and she made herself a promise that if he blew her off she was done chasing the delicious Joe Harris.

"Okay. If you're sure it's not a problem."

She grinned, cocking her head to look up at him. "Tate cooks enough for an army. One more person won't hurt. Heck, she'll be thrilled. Because she's weird that way."

He reached out and took her hand, bringing it to his mouth to kiss. "I really am sorry about last night."

"Me too. I hope everything is okay now. With your family I mean."

He sighed again. "Yeah."

She gave him Tate's address and told him she'd see him at

seven for dinner. He walked her to her car and frowned when she started it.

"When's the last time you had a tune-up?"

She shrugged. "I don't know. It's running fine."

He bent, and she leaned out to kiss him because he looked so good. "Don't try to change the subject."

She laughed. "Am I so transparent?"

"Bring it by the shop on Monday morning. Leave it and it'll be done by the time you get off work."

"You're being very nice to me."

"I like you." He stood before he said anything else, stepping back. "See you at seven."

Chapter Seven

She watched Joe, his head bent toward William, a huge grin on his face.

"I think he's good for William." Tate handed Beth a cream soda. "It's good for him to have friends around. I admit when Joe first came to town I wasn't convinced he'd outgrown his past."

"I feel like we're talking about one of the kids." Beth sipped her soda. "Maybe we should have Joe over for a playdate."

"If so, can I play with him too?" Anne waggled her brows and Beth threw a piece of ice at her. A little harder than she needed to.

"Ouch! I was just joking."

Beth giggled. "I laugh because it hurts. Remember that. Keep your mitts away."

Anne gave her a surreptitious middle finger. "I've never seen you actually jealous before. It's fascinating. You're going to get a line on your forehead though, so stop. He's too tall for my taste. But he's got a great ass."

"He's the kind of kisser that makes a woman weak in the knees. Takes his time." She shivered as she watched him with her brothers and the Chase boys.

"Man takes his time with your mouth, he's good with other

parts." Tate looked wistfully over in her husband's direction.

"You all should remember I am single at the moment. I'm not getting any and all this talk is making me antsy." Anne sighed.

"Then why do you keep turning Royal down when he asks you to marry him?" Maggie Chase asked.

But Beth knew the answer. Anne had grown up smacked in the face with the worst marriage ever. Their parents were miserable people on their own. Together they'd been a train wreck of epic proportions. Anne didn't believe any marriage could work. And Beth also knew despite how beautiful, smart and talented her sister was, she didn't believe she was worthy of her happily ever after.

So she held men back. Royal was the one who kept at it. But he was close to giving up and that made Beth sad. He was a good man who loved her sister. But the scars your life gives you sometimes run so deep you can't ever heal over.

In the end, she just wasn't sure Royal had whatever it took to get past Anne's defenses. Or if anyone did.

Anne sighed. "I don't want to get married. If he'd just date me, we'd be fine. But he insists on marriage and I keep telling him I'm not interested."

Beth neatly stepped in and changed the subject. "So, Tate, what do you think? Boy or girl this time?"

The sisters looked over, laughing and whispering. Matt Chase raised a brow and looked to Joe. "They're talking about you."

Joe felt the heat of a blush. "What makes you say that?"

"He's not a moron." William sat back and sipped his soda.

"Don't look so panicked. They do it about us all." Matt

tipped his glass. "Thank God for it. Look at 'em."

The group took the women in. Marc Chase, Matt's little brother, laughed. "Damn, such a pretty bunch of females. Each is wily though, Joe. That's the thing. Beauty, no doubt. But they're all smart and independent."

"They work in a pack." That was Shane, the sheriff and oldest Chase brother.

That made Joe laugh. "A pack?"

"Wolves are really smart. And vicious as hell if you mess with them and theirs."

"I like Beth. Beth likes me. That's really it." He shrugged. "I've known you Murphys for my entire life. She's a friend first and foremost."

It was Marc who seemed to find that the funniest. "Yeah. Liv and I were friends too. Now she's given me two babies and makes me mow the lawn."

Yeah well hopefully she wouldn't have to call their children to come over to talk him down from a rage where he'd threatened to burn the house down with their mother in it. That had been a great capper to a night where he thought he'd be getting in between Beth's thighs.

He'd dropped Beth off and raced to his parents' house to find his mother huddling in the car, weeping, while his father paced around the house, ranting and making threats.

There was a dark knot of rage in his father's belly and it seemed to be growing. Joe had no idea what to do about it. He wanted to call the cops, hoping that the shock would push his father to get help. But his mother had only gotten more upset. Joe had brought her to his apartment to spend the night, but she'd gone home soon after she'd gotten up and kept insisting things were fine.

He shouldn't have come here. But Beth had been so pretty when she asked. So sweet. And the allure of normal time with friends was too much to turn down. It had been good, he realized. He'd needed it. But he knew it wasn't a good idea to get used to it.

But it was hard to keep to that when she'd sat with him while they watched the movie. One of the kids snuggled up in her lap with Buck, who everyone had insisted he bring over, who'd laid his head on her thigh. She spent a lot of her time laughing and joking.

He noticed she filled that spot in her family. She made it look effortless, the way she cheered up crying children. He'd watched her steer the conversation around potential arguments between her siblings, even as she'd defended them, and in a few cases, delivered a little discipline.

And there they sat in his truck, in his driveway because Buck was with them. He should have dropped her off first, then he'd have a way to just kiss her and move on. He *knew* once they had sex things would deepen between them. How could they not? He should avoid it.

He gave himself this lecture as she chatted with Buck, who'd managed to claim her lap. Whatever it was, Buck thought it was awesome because he gave her his best dog grin and licked her here and there to underline it.

Joe didn't blame Buck. He wanted to lick her too.

He got out and went around, and she handed him the dog first, before he helped her out.

"He's spoiled enough as it is."

She laughed. "The kids were in heaven with him tonight. I'm so glad you came along, Buck. You made lots of happy giggly children."

Buck danced to the front door after he stopped to sniff

around the steps and the flowerboxes. He snorted, peed on a few places and barreled into the house when Joe opened the door.

"So, Joe Harris, are *you* going to make this girl all giggly?"

He backed her up against the wall, pressing himself into her body. "I think so, yeah." He kissed her slow, tasting her, settling in. "Though your mouth might be too busy to giggle."

"You say the hottest stuff."

Her hands made their way under the hem of his shirt, stroking up his back, nails scoring lightly, sending shivers through him.

"I really want to see those tattoos."

He picked her up and headed back to his bedroom. Once he'd tossed her to his bed, he pulled his shirt up and over his head, reveling in the way she looked him over.

"Good God," she breathed out. "I might come just from looking at you."

"Don't leave without me." He pulled her pretty sandals off, digging his thumbs in, kneading until she made a sound that shot straight to his cock.

The hem of the skirt she wore slid up, exposing a whole lot of tanned thigh. He knelt on the bed, sliding his palms up from her ankles, up her calves, pausing to dig his thumbs in just behind her knee. Her lips parted on a soft sigh as she watched him.

She parted her thighs, giving him a glimpse of fire-engine-red panties. Her cleavage heaved up at the scoop neck of the shirt she had on. He shook his head. "There's so much here I don't know where to start. You're like Christmas and my birthday all in one ridiculously sexy package."

"You can start by getting rid of your shorts."

She smiled. *That* smile.

His hands went to his waist, and she watched, her breath catching as he popped the button.

"You should get rid of that shirt." He tipped his chin in her direction.

She sat up, crisscrossed her arms, grabbed her shirt at the hem and pulled it off, leaving her in a sexy red bra.

He ran covetous hands all over her then. Needing to touch that soft, pretty skin. Needing the curve of her breasts.

"Damn, baby, you're so pretty." He brushed his lips over the right breast and then the left as he got her bra unhooked and pulled away from her upper body.

He sucked in a breath. "These. Sweet baby Jesus." He thumbed across her nipples until she squeaked, arching into him, her fingers clutching his biceps to keep him close.

"When you had on a shirt and sandals, the skirt was sexy, but pretty wholesome." He sat back on his heels to take her in. Tousled. Lips swollen from his kisses, her hair had come loose from the ponytail she'd been wearing. Her tits, holy shit, perfect, pert B cups.

"And now?"

"Now." He reached up under her skirt and pulled her panties—a tiny scrap of red fabric—off. "Now somehow that skirt looks ridiculously sexy."

"Your shorts are still on."

He'd been in mid-strip when she'd taken her shirt off. "Like you can blame me? Your tits are so hot I just sort of forgot everything else."

She reared up, grabbing his shorts and boxers, pulling them down. "Oh. My." He tried not to blush as he got everything off and settled back on the bed with her.

She scrambled atop his body, running her hands all over his chest. Tracing over his tattoos. "These are amazing."

He looked down at the barbed wire created with gears. "I traded labor with a tattoo artist. He needed help overhauling an engine. I wanted some ink."

She bent, her hair sliding over his chest as she pressed a kiss against it. She licked over each of his nipples until he grunted, shifting.

Her pussy rested against his cock. Hot. Wet. She undulated, brushing herself against him, and he groaned. "I want in you so much my teeth hurt."

She caught her bottom lip between straight, white teeth. "Yeah? What are you waiting for then?"

He flipped her to her back. "There are other things I want to do first." He kissed her belly and then up. Up to the curve of her breast, just beneath, leading up to her nipple, which he swirled a tongue around until she arched on a gasp.

He was so big. Tall. Shoulders wide. Burnished by the sun. Strengthened by hard work. His hands were work rough, but gentle as he touched her. She liked big men. Tall, long, workstrong. This man was all that and more.

It was the *and more* part that made her weak in the knees. He leaned over her body, his cock hard, insistent at her thigh. His mouth cruised over her skin, totally sure.

His body was so gorgeous she couldn't stand it. Inside her head she squealed with delight. All that ink on his chest and upper arms matched the wary eyes and the too-long blond hair. He was a big, bad man but only on the outside.

Lordamighty that was hot. The hottest thing she'd ever been this close to.

She *really* liked it.

He drew on her nipple, sucking tight until she made a sound she hadn't even intended on making. He chuckled. A cocksure guy sound. A shiver went through her.

Never, ever in her life had she been more turned on. And that was before he reversed his movement, heading down. Kissing over her ribs, across each hipbone and around her belly button.

Then, as he held her gaze, he pushed her skirt up and broke her gaze, looking down at her pussy with such raw hunger she had to swallow back a moan at the sight.

"Can I tell you something?" he murmured, his lips so close that she felt the puffs of air against her labia. She nodded, wordless. "I love this part of a woman."

He spread her open and bent his head to take a long lick.

"I'm glad to hear it," she managed to say around a tongue that felt too big for her mouth.

"I'm going to lick you until you come so hard you can't speak. And then I'm going to fuck you."

She had no words already so she gave him two thumbs-up and kept watching, sifting her fingers through his hair.

He certainly seemed to love this part of her. Over and over he teased her with his lips. With his tongue and fingers, and every once in a while, the edge of his teeth. He took it slow. So achingly slow she thought she'd explode from it.

And when it came, when orgasm sucked her under, her back bowed as she tried not to pull his hair too hard, holding him in place as wave after wave of pleasure hit her.

But she wasn't so boneless she wasn't able to grab his cock when he tried to move up and past her.

He started to speak until she gave the head of his cock a lick, then the words dissolved into a groan. He stilled, letting her have her way as she licked up the line of him and sucked.

He was a big man. In more ways than one. She had no trouble paying homage to his cock. Cupping his balls as she licked around the crown. He moaned softly, saying her name a few times.

He cradled her head, stroking his free hand over her hair. "Yes, God, yes." She kept on until he pulled her hair, sending a delighted wave of sensation over her skin from the scalp down. "Enough. For now."

She pulled off and flopped back to the mattress with a pout.

He kissed her quickly. "Don't pout." He returned in moments with a foil square and tore it open with his teeth. Anticipation sliced through her as she couldn't tear her gaze from the sight of him rolling the latex over his cock, suiting up.

"On your hands and knees." He turned her. "Facing the mirror so I can watch."

He was totally going to kill her with the dirty stuff.

He got behind her, on his knees and watched the long line of her back. He spread her thighs and teased her with the head of his cock until she was nearly insane and pushed back, taking the head of him inside.

He put a staying, slowing hand on her hip. "Shhh. It's coming." She was so tight he needed to go slow. He didn't want to hurt her, and he was already so close to coming that if she took him any quicker it would be over before it really got started.

She hummed, a sort of moan, as her fingers tangled in the comforter. Her eyes were closed, so it left him free to look at other parts of her. The ones he saw reflected in the mirror—the sway of those tits as he pressed in deeper and then deeper, the way her lips parted on a sigh when he reached around and gave her clit a feather-light touch. And the ones laid out before him like a buffet. The silky-smooth skin of her back. The curve of her ass. The definition of her biceps as she moved. The sable-dark hair as it slid over her shoulders.

She was the most beautiful thing he'd ever had in his bed, definitely the most beautiful woman he'd ever been inside of.

"More," she gasped. "Please."

She swiveled her hips a bit, making him see spots as he locked his jaw and concentrated. He pulled her hips back as he pressed in, just a little. And then a little more.

She was inferno hot. Hot enough to scald him even through the condom. So tight, sweat beaded on his forehead as he struggled to keep control.

"You feel so good," she whispered and it tore at his heart. At the walls he built around himself. This woman was so honest, so raw. It made the sex a million times better, but also left him stripped down.

That she seemed to enjoy fucking as much as he did was a good thing. He needed to stop tripping on the other stuff that didn't matter. He shook his head, sliding in that last bit. This was hot. She was hot. There was no reason not to enjoy every last moment of it.

He began to stroke, fucking her slow and deep. She kept his pace, pressing back with that swivel of hers. Over and over until he wasn't sure where he ended and she began. Until he found that place of no return.

He reached around again, finding her slick, her clit swollen to his touch. He slid a fingertip over it and around it. In time with his strokes until her inner walls fluttered, tightened around him, sucking a gasp from his lips as she came. Dragging him right along with her as orgasm hit him so hard his skin tingled as he groaned long and low. It went on and on until he collapsed beside her, finding his muscle control enough to get up to rid himself of the condom and return to her again.

She smiled at him, leaning to kiss his elbow as it was right next to her face. "Wow. If you can fix a car half as well as you can sex a girl up, you're going to make a million dollars."

He laughed, pulling her closer. "I'll take that compliment quite gracefully. Though admittedly you certainly made it all worthwhile."

Buck bumped the door Joe had closed on the way in earlier.

"My dog has a crush on you."

She snorted. "He's awfully cute. Like his human."

He sat. "I'm hungry again."

"I may need those promised Epsom salts first."

He laughed harder. "I meant for actual food. Meet me in the kitchen and I'll make it worth your while."

Chapter Eight

Joe stepped in between his father and their neighbor, ending the yelling. "Mr. Pierson, I surely do apologize. I'll get this handled today." He steered his father away, though his father resisted.

"Get your hands off me, boy!"

"Do you want to go to jail?" Joe was a man in the prime of his life while his father had been battling injuries and illness for the last three decades. It wasn't hard to get him to go where Joe wanted.

But his father was on a tear. Angry words fell from his mouth like rain. "You think you can be gone for ten years and just come back and everything is all right? I can take care of my own business."

Joe gently, but firmly pushed his father inside, closing and locking the door, standing between his father and any escape.

"You don't have anything handled."

His mother sighed, wringing her hands. "Carl, be easy now. Joe's just trying to help."

"He's useless. It's a wonder he's here and not in prison."

Joe took a deep breath. "The Joe who left here ten years ago could have easily ended up in prison. But I'm not that dumb kid anymore. I've changed. I'm hoping you'll let me show you that. But in the meantime, you can't start fights with the neighbors. You're going to get the cops called and then what?"

"I can store my trash any damned way I see fit!"

"No, you can't. You're in the city limits and there are laws about how you deal with your trash. You know that. Pierson knows that. I'll get the trash dealt with in a few minutes. I've got the truck, I'll take it to the dump."

"I don't need you to take my trash out!"

"You need someone to tell you a few things." Joe had made some calls over the last week. His own status as a vet had helped a little. He had some resources on hand. He knew his father had been blowing up more and more, almost always over his stuff and anyone touching it or trying to get him to deal with it. There were issues here far more than the slipped discs in his back.

"Oh yeah? And you think you're the man to do it?"

He sighed. "Dad, sit down, please. I don't want to fight with you. But this has gone far enough. It's a serious thing, you know. People are starting to talk. You're upsetting people, including Mom."

"Why is it anyone's business?" The rage had washed away now, the confusion replacing it.

"It's not until your stuff spills into your neighbor's driveway. Or when you start a fight with the mail carrier or George down at the hardware store. Or when you scare my mother. There's something wrong and I think it's time to see someone."

"There's not a damned thing wrong with me!"

"Dad, you run off in your pajamas with no shoes on. You start fights with the neighbors. Heck, with your friends. People you've known for decades. You forget what you're saying halfway through a sentence. You say things...hateful, ugly things that I know you don't mean. You threatened to burn the house down with Mom inside. You're not that man. Sometimes your chemistry gets mixed up. It's like dirty gasoline. It messes up everything, building up until things break down little by little. It's not your fault. But you don't have to keep suffering. There are things to help."

"You don't know anything about me. You left."

Joe nodded. "I did. I know I was a crappy son. I know I kept you awake with worry lots of nights. I'm not that person anymore. I'm here to help. I made some calls. I know you don't want to go to Atlanta. But there are some other places we can start that are closer to home. All we need to get started is you saying yes."

"I'm not crazy."

"Of course you're not crazy. No one is saying that."

"Then what *are* you saying?"

Joe sucked in a breath and hoped like hell he was going to do this right. "I'm saying that your behavior isn't normal. Not for you. This stuff you're doing, it's getting worse. Your brain chemistry might be off. They have medication that can help. I'm saying I'd like you to make an appointment to see someone about it. Just a first step and we can go from there. You're not crazy. There is help. If you'll just take it. There's nothing to be ashamed of."

"I'll think about it." His dad got up and left the room.

Beside Joe, his mother let out a sigh. "You handled that well. Thank you. He doesn't mean all that, you know. You weren't a crappy son."

"Yeah? If I wasn't, why'd it take you so long to call to ask me for help?"

"Oh, honey. You have made something for yourself. You made us proud when you went into the army. Worried, of course, especially when you were in Iraq so long. But then you came back and you got a job and you built a life for yourself. I didn't want to mess that up. You and your sister deserve lives away from here."

He put an arm around her shoulders. "Petal's not so bad. The garage is doing well. I just hired another mechanic and a part-timer." And Beth, things were going well with her too. "My best friends live here. You and Dad are here. We'll get through this. I've got to go make a run to the dump. You gonna be all right?"

She nodded. "He'll hole up in the shed a few hours. When he erupts, he usually will be okay for a day or two until the next time."

"I'll be back later today to check in."

He backed his truck up and filled it with the bags of garbage that had spilled into the driveway next door. Mr. Pierson watched him carefully for a while, but once he was assured Joe was dealing with it like he'd promised, he'd gone away.

The incidents were getting closer together.

There was no way around that. His father's mental state was eroding. His anger was worse, and Joe was concerned that his father would end up hurting someone.

Where his dad had always had anger in him, he hadn't been quick with his fists. That had been Joe's thing. He'd gotten what he'd later thought of as rage hangovers. All that physical anger had washed through him until he couldn't see straight or think right. The army had given him the discipline to divert that, to channel his energy so that he could deal with his shit without his fists. The last thing he wanted was for his father to wake up, fully cognizant of the mess he'd made, the things he'd done that were not something he could take back.

The years of drinking might have taken a toll on him. Certainly it had masked some of the symptoms as he self-medicated.

The woman at the mental-health-services line had given Joe a great list of resources. He'd read a lot on the internet as well. There were many things this could be. But none of it was anything they could treat unless and until he got in to see someone capable of diagnosing whatever it was.

So that was step one.

He was a better man than the shit-headed kid who'd signed up for the military because he'd been drunk and jingoistic. He'd learned a lot. Become a man. And he needed to show his father that he was someone worth leaning on.

Beth had her hands in the dirt. Digging and planting. Around her the kids played. Some of them helped. The little ones wandered off with the flowers and would bring them back occasionally.

It was a good day there in Tate's front yard.

Tate sat nearby in a chair Matt had brought out for her. He'd even glowered at his wife until she'd sighed and sat. Then he'd put up an umbrella to shield her from the sun, and people had come by continually to freshen her lemonade or tea.

This pregnancy had been harder on her than the other two. The early months, she'd been fine with occasional evening nausea. But after she'd moved into the second trimester, she'd been so sick in the early parts of the day she'd actually lost weight.

The baby was fine. Growing well. So that was good. Tate was at the stage where she cried a lot, which was normal too. But Beth hated to see her sister in any sort of discomfort.

They all did.

Family had simply gathered around her in a protective knot. Of course that had driven Tate, who was used to being the one in charge, insane. Which was just too bad because people loved her too damned much to let her be any more uncomfortable than she had to be.

But it was nice having Tate all to herself for a bit. It'd been a while since they'd been able to really visit.

Tate must have felt the same. "So what's going on with you lately? I feel like between the salon and me not being there every day and the pregnancy and your new man, that we don't touch base enough. I've neglected you and I'm sorry."

Beth rolled her eyes at her sister. "We talk every day. You're busy. That's how it works when you have two kids under five and another on the way. I'm busy because we're taking up the slack. That's also how it works. When I get married and have babies, you'll do the same for me."

Elizabeth or "Lil Beth" toddled over, handing her mother a clump of dirt, and then plopped down in Beth's lap.

"Hi."

Beth smiled, kissing the top of her head, in between two little pigtails of pale blonde hair just like her momma's. "Hi there, lumpkin. You brought some dirt to momma?"

Lil Beth nodded with a grin.

"Did you by any chance eat some of that dirt too?"

She shook her head, but Matt loped over. "Mmm hmmm. What did daddy say about eating dirt?"

"No!" But that she said it as she kicked her feet and leaned back into Beth while laughing sort of spoiled the admonishment.

Tate grinned, shaking her head.

Beth stood, holding Lil Beth on her hip. "How about we go inside and wash faces and brush teeth?"

"I can do that." Matt held his hands out but Lil Beth held on to her aunt tighter.

"We've got this one." Beth smiled and gave a quick head jerk toward Tate who was looking green around the edges.

He held a hand out to his wife and looked at her with so much adoration that Beth squeezed the baby to her a little tighter as she took her inside. "All right you, come inside. Everything is done anyway. Jacob just ran to grab pizza, but there's some rice left over if you'd rather have something plain. Maybe with some fruit? You need to eat, Venus."

"Your daddy sure does love your momma. Which is good, because you have the best momma in the whole wide world. You know, I think maybe a bath might be good too. What do you think, stinkbug?"

Lil Beth, who was pretty much the happiest baby Beth had ever seen, just giggled and nodded.

Once inside, half the family set about getting food ready so she moved toward the girls' bedroom at the back of the house and the bathroom to get some babies clean.

Beth set the baby down while she got the water temp just right and began to fill the tub. Lil Beth started stripping down, making Beth laugh.

"Need some help there, stinkbug?"

She sat, her arms halfway out of her little shirt. "Yes!"

Beth helped her, tossing the dirty clothes in the nearby hamper.

"Meg, my darlin, you coming?" she called out, knowing how much these girls loved the bathtub.

"Here, Aunt Beth!" Meg bounded into the room naked as a jaybird.

"Want bubbles?"

"Yes, ma'am!"

"Can you help sissy choose a nightgown?"

Meg nodded and ran into the other room to help her sister find a nightgown to change into.

Nathan cruised past. "Everything okay? Can I help?"

"I'm just going to get the girls cleaned up and dressed for bed. Be sure Tate is sitting."

"Matt's on that."

Meg streaked in, putting two nightgowns on the counter.

Nathan snorted. "Girl, you have no clothes on!" He covered his eyes with a hand and Meg thought that was hilarious. He was quick enough to grab a diaperless Lil Beth as she attempted to toddle past. He deposited her in the bathtub and Meg followed.

"I'm going to leave you to it. Mind your aunt, girls."

By the time she'd finished, Beth had to change her shirt because she'd gotten soaked from two giggling girls. But there was something so sweet about freshly bathed babies in princess nightgowns she didn't mind one bit.

Moments like this one, days like that day were Beth's life now. So wonderful. Filled with so many people she loved.

They'd never had that growing up. Never had adults fighting over who got to take them for an overnight or who brought them bubbles to blow just because. Certainly never had pretty pink princess nightgowns.

That generation of Murphy kids had a damned good life. William's kids, Tim's kids, Tate's kids—all loved, all being raised with a firm, guiding hand. They didn't have to be what they came from. Just thinking about it that way loosened the knot of anxiety that lived in her belly that she had the seeds to be her mother inside her. Or worse, their father.

Her siblings had divested her of that fear on a rational level. She could see them as husbands and wives, as parents, and know they were so much more than those hellish years in that trailer could have made them.

"You all right?" Tate asked as Beth settled in with a big slice of pizza. The girls were at the table eating pizza and laughing like crazy with their dad and Uncle Nathan.

"This gonna bug you?" Beth indicated the pizza. It smelled heavenly to her, but she wasn't pregnant.

"Nah, I'm all right. Matt went and got me some of that ginger-brew stuff. The real goods. I had one and I feel much better. Though I'm going to start burping like a sailor because of the carbonation. Thanks for getting the girls cleaned up."

"No problem. You know I love to help, and they're so freaking adorable it's not a chore at all."

"I'm biased, but honestly, two more adorable baby girls I have yet to see. Now, you're going to tell me why you had that look on your face."

"Nothing bad. I was just thinking about how these kids teach me that we're more than what we came from. You're an amazing mother. I mean, I know that because you're basically *my* mother. But when Matt approaches, they don't run away. They don't flinch. They turn to him, little faces turned up to him expectantly. They run to him when he comes in from work. They make noise and caper around, and they aren't afraid. They have things simply because those things make them happy. Not in an overabundance, you and Matt are smart about not spoiling them too much. You, William and Tim have created a new generation of Murphys who seem to have escaped any marks from what we were. It's a good thing."

Tate sat there, tears running down her face. "Everyone's gonna ignore me because of course I cry at cotton commercials now. But what you just said? It's the nicest, most wonderful thing. Thank you. I love you so much, Beth. I'm so glad you're in my life. So glad you're in my daughters' lives too. How are things with Joe?"

Beth shrugged. "Good. I don't see him a lot. Like once a week or so. Maybe twice. We text and email. He's got something going on at home. I wager it's about his father. I've heard stuff around town. But he hasn't shared much."

Beth got it. More than she wanted to really. She understood being closed up about stuff that happened at home. Understood shame. "I get it. I do. He's not ready to share."

"But you want him to. William told me there was trouble at home too, but he wasn't saying much. I don't think Joe has told him anything either."

"It's not like boys really do that sort of sharing anyway. I do hope, for his sake, that he's got someone to talk to though. It's hard to manage stuff alone."

"There's gossip. About Carl I mean. He's been starting fights. Unusual."

"I heard. I'm wary about bringing it up so I haven't."

"I think you're probably right. Let me ask you this though. Is he worth it? I mean, sure he's hesitant to share, but that's what people who're in a relationship do. They share their troubles and their triumphs too."

"We're dating. That's all for now. He's busy. I'm busy. We see each other when we get the chance. As long as he's not seeing anyone else when he's got the chance, we're all right. I like him. A lot. He's strong. He's got a good heart. Love that dog of his. Man who'd treat a dog like that is a good man."

Tate nodded. "I tend to agree. I just want you to be happy. I want him to be worthy of you."

She grinned at her sister, putting her head on Tate's shoulder a moment. "Me too. I want him to share. I want to earn his trust. For now, where we are is all right. I'm taking it one day at a time."

"That's fair." Tate tipped her chin toward where Matt sat with his daughters. "I just want you to have that too."

"Oh so do I. I wondered if I'd ever be ready for such a thing, and more and more lately I'm totally sure I am. I want a passel of babies and a husband. I want to plant flowers out in front of my house and I want my babies' daddy to tease them about eating dirt."

"You'll have it. I know you will. Matt changed everything. I had no idea really. I never expected that sort of fidelity and constancy. It's the most wonderful thing in the world to share this with him. I can't wait for you to have that as well."

"He's only been back a few months. Things are going slow and that's okay. For now."

He missed her.

Joe glanced at the salon as he closed up the garage and headed home. It had been nearly a week since he'd seen her last. They'd spoken here and there, but he wanted to touch her. To hear her voice as she was right next to him instead of over a phone.

He'd convinced his father to go see someone. They'd had an

appointment just two days before and were waiting to hear back. It gave him some measure of comfort, though waiting was tough now, with the promise of some relief just over the next rise. Maybe.

He paused in his driveway. Pulling his phone out to text her.

You around?

He waited a few moments until she replied.

I am. How are you?

There's a distinct Beth-shaped spot in my life and it's empty. Wanna fill it?

A pause.

Is this a booty call, Mr. Harris?

He snorted a laugh and Buck barked.

I was thinking about a slice of pie at the Sands first.

Pie? Why didn't you say so? I'll be waiting for you to pick me up.

Your wish is my command.

He got Buck out of the car and into the house. He needed to brush his teeth and his hair too.

His phone pinged one last time. A picture she'd taken of herself with one brow raised. The accompanying text said, *Oh yeah? After pie. My commands will be a lot nicer then.*

She was waiting for him, her hair up in a high ponytail, face with only a trace of makeup. As they were moving toward fall, it was still warm in the evenings, but not stiflingly hot any longer. Gone were most of the shorts and tank tops women had worn so often. She wore a skirt though. He loved her legs, so he wasn't complaining.

"Hello there, Mizz Murphy."

She looked him up from his toes to his face. A smile on her lips. "My goodness you're even better than pie."

That deserved a kiss.

But when he pulled her close and brought his mouth to hers, it wasn't a quick hello. He was drawn in to that sweetness of her lips. The lushness of her mouth. Her taste.

He'd been inside her. More than once. Had kissed all the best parts of her. And he still yearned for more.

He finally pulled away, nearly going back again when she licked her lips as if to get one last taste.

"Come on then. Before I forget about pie and ravish you right here on the doorstep."

"Like that's incentive to leave?"

He tugged her toward his truck. "I need to eat. The calories will help me do what I have planned for you."

She laughed and let him help her up into the truck.

It wasn't all that far to the Sands, and it was already eight so a parking space on Main was suitably quick to find as well. They grabbed a booth and sat.

"I want a cup of decaf and some peach cobbler, please."

Joe ordered some chicken, potatoes, greens, a slice of pie and a salad.

"What have you been up to this week?"

"The shop has been crazy busy. Which is good." And true because they weren't sure just how much of his father's treatment would be covered by the insurance he had, and Joe didn't want his dad to hesitate because he was worried about cost.

"My car is running a lot smoother since you did whatever you did to it."

He loved to watch her eat. Beth Murphy didn't hide how much she enjoyed whatever it was she was doing. She ate her cobbler, loving each and every bite she took.

"What? Do you want a bite?"

He laughed. "Nope. I've got my own pie coming after my dinner. Just having a great time watching you eat yours. I saw William yesterday. He said Tate's been under the weather?"

"She had two pretty easy pregnancies. This one? Not so much. The baby is fine. Which takes a big weight off her shoulders. But she's really sick and having a hard time eating. She's tired too. We're all taking turns with the kids. Polly Chase has been amazing as well. She adores Tate, of course, and you can only imagine what sort of grandma she is to those girls. Anyway Tate, being Tate, hates it when she thinks anyone is being put out on her behalf. So she frets and fusses when anyone helps. And that pisses everyone off because hello, Tate has been doing for all of us our whole lives."

His food arrived, and he noticed when Royal Watson and Nathan came in. Royal came over. "Hey, Joe, what's going on these days?" He grinned. "It's my favorite Murphy sister."

"You and Anne off again?"

Joe realized it would be rude not to invite them to sit, so he did, giving Beth an apologetic glance. Her response told him she wasn't mad. She scooted over to allow Nathan to sit on her side.

"How'd you know?" Royal asked as he settled in.

"Duh. If you were on again, I'd be your second favorite."

Nathan grabbed a spoon and Beth rapped him on the knuckles. "Not even. Get your own cobbler."

"You're mean."

"Yeah, that's me. Where's your girlfriend?"

"If I didn't know better, I'd think you liked Lily more than me. Which would make me sad."

"Course I like her better. I can borrow her clothes. However, you'll always be my favorite Nathan in the whole world. If there was only enough cobbler left for one, I'd share. But the case is full. Therefore, you can get your own."

"She and Chris are having a phone call with their mom. I thought it was best I not be around." He shrugged. "She'll feel better when they've checked in. Pamela is getting better. It's good. It makes Lily happy, it keeps Chris on a good path."

"Glad to hear it. You still need to order your own cobbler though. I'll even pay for it."

Her brother snorted. "Stingy."

"When it comes to baked goods, your sister is definitely not a sharer." Joe winked at her.

Nathan shook his head. "She'd give you a kidney. But not her cobbler."

"Tate raised me right. Sheesh."

Royal and Nathan ordered some food. She'd hoped for a nice intimate dinner, just her and Joe, but really, it was nice to hang out with friends too. Like an actual couple.

People stopped by the booth to check in on Tate. To say hey to Joe or one of the others. It was a normal night in Petal. One that made Beth happy she lived in a small town and knew most everyone.

Of course there were the women who looked at Joe a little too long. But he was there with her so it didn't matter. Or the ones who tried to get Nathan's attention, which pissed her off because he was getting married and everyone in town knew it.

Nathan pretended not to notice. But he wasn't clueless like some men who were as handsome as he was. It just didn't matter to him because Lily was everything he'd ever wanted.

Royal got his share of attention too. One of these days he was going to give up on Anne and some other woman was going to snap him up and Anne would finally figure it out like a dumbass. But it would be too late.

"You two have hogged all my time with Beth." Joe said this after he'd eaten.

Nathan gave him a look. "Your time, huh?"

She stepped on his foot extra hard.

"Hey, Joe." Clancy Weeks approached the table and Beth noted how Joe tightened up.

"Clancy."

"Listen, I hate to do this but—"

Joe held a hand up to stop the conversation. "Let's take this outside."

Beth looked to Nathan for a moment, alarmed there was going to be a fight or something. But there didn't seem to be any anger from Clancy.

Royal scooted out to let Joe up. Joe turned to Beth. "I'll be right back."

She wanted to ask him if everything was all right, but Nathan poked her side hard enough that she figured that was a bad idea.

Royal and Nathan had some silent guy conversation with eyebrows and facial expressions until she finally broke in. "Hello? What? Do we need to call the cops or something?"

"I can see them from where I am. They're just talking. In case you haven't noticed, Joe's a big boy. Let him handle his business."

She frowned at Nathan. "Oh really? I had no idea. I figured he needed his girlfriend to go out there and handle it. Don't treat me like I'm stupid."

But it wouldn't kill the man to actually tell her what was going on. Clearly Nathan knew something, and while she got that right then wasn't the place, it would be nice to have someone share something.

Joe waited until the door had closed and they'd gotten a bit away before he stopped, turning to Clancy. "What's this all about?"

"Come on, Joe. You know or you'd have talked to me inside. It's Carl. I've tried to reason with him. I've tried to talk to him. To threaten him even. But he won't listen. It's worse each time he comes in now. I have no other choice. Your dad can't come in the store anymore. I'm sorry but every time he does, he makes trouble. Tries to start fights. He scares people. I can't have that."

Joe ran a hand through his hair. The hardware store was one of his dad's favorite places. It was going to crush him not to be able to go there. But Joe got it. If half of what he heard was true, it was a miracle his dad hadn't been arrested by then. Maybe he could use that to keep his father invested in the treatment plan when they got one.

"No, I understand. I'll let him know. You can call me at the shop." He pulled out a business card and handed it over. "If he comes in and I'll get him."

"I'm sorry, Joe. He's been a customer—and a friend—for a long time. But he needs help."

Joe weighed talking with Clancy, but knew his father would be livid. He settled on, "I know. We're working on it. Appreciate you coming to me instead of calling the cops."

Clancy started to speak but stopped himself. Instead he nodded and left Joe alone on the sidewalk. Joe turned to look inside. Beth sat with Nathan and Royal. He caught sight of her giving Nathan the stinkeye about something and it cheered him up.

Feisty, his Beth.

His.

He paused and realized it was true.

He needed her. Needed to work up a sweat and get rid of this exchange with Clancy. He suffocated from the weight of everything he was responsible for. The stakes were so high he was petrified of fucking it up.

But Beth let him be. Gave him what he needed, demanded but never what he couldn't give. Each time they were together he drew closer to her. Tenacious, his Beth. She'd wanted him and it had been incredible to be chased. But now it was he who craved her just as much. It was Beth who filled his empty spots in a way he'd gotten used to.

He'd tried so hard not to need her that it had happened while he wasn't looking. Another thing to be petrified of. He wanted her. A great deal. And for the moment, he let himself, heading back inside.

Chapter Nine

"Can I come in?"

She turned to him. "Yes."

"I can't stay. Overnight I mean. I need to get home to Buck and I have to be at the shop at seven. I…"

She saw need all over him. Not just sexual need. She filled something inside him that was empty and that was enough for then.

She unlocked her door, and he followed, locking up behind himself.

He backed her against the wall, right there in her entry, his mouth on hers, taking. She gave, tiptoeing to meet his mouth, pressing herself against him because he filled something inside her too. Need was a fire on her skin as those big hands roved over her body.

He kissed down her neck, pausing where neck met shoulder. He licked the skin there and she couldn't stop the tremble. Couldn't stop herself from any physical response he elicited. He played her body, knew what she liked and where she liked it.

He broke away to pull her shirt off and rid her of her bra. He brushed himself against her, the cotton of his shirt against her bare skin made her writhe at the sensation.

"You're so sexy. It's all I think about. All week long. Fixing a carburetor, changing oil, doesn't matter. Your body, the way you taste, goddamn I can't get you out of my head."

She sucked in a breath, both at the feel of his mouth on her nipple and the words. He stripped her raw, bare.

She managed to grab his shirt and pull it up. Hissing at the feel of his skin against hers. Hot and taut. She'd wanted this all week. Had thought of it over and over. Just as he had, apparently.

She was wet and achy. Drowning in a need no one had ever evoked this way before.

Her nails dug into the muscle at his back, urging him forward.

Then he dropped to his knees, pressing his face into her belly as his hands skimmed up her calves and thighs until he reached her underpants, pulling them down and off as she stepped from them.

She leaned against the wall, watching down her body as he pushed her skirt up and parted her, taking a long lick, all while his gaze was locked on hers. Watching her watch him.

"I love the way you taste."

She managed to gasp as he held her labia open with his thumbs, licking her until the only thing holding her up were his hands and the wall at her back.

She came so hard and fast it consumed her until there was nothing but the place his hands touched, nothing but where he'd kissed her thigh. He stood and picked her up like it was easy, carrying her to her bedroom.

"Now that I've taken the edge off I can take my time," he murmured as he got the rest of his clothes off.

"But my edge was the one taken off." She grinned up at

him.

"You clearly underestimate how hot it is to watch you fly apart, darlin'. I'm going to fuck you now."

He said it as he tore a condom packet open, rolling it on his cock as he climbed to the bed.

She got to her knees, grabbing his cock at the root. "You're stingy with this." Leaning close, she licked over the nipple closest to her, and he arched with a hiss.

"Am not. I'm planning on letting you have it as soon as you climb on top. I want *in* your pussy right now."

She groaned at the power of his words. "I want this in my mouth."

He cupped her throat with his palm. So much power in that hand, he could have easily harmed her. But he didn't. He held her there as he plundered her mouth.

He didn't feel like this. Not while fucking—and God knew he loved sex and had had it with all sorts of women. Not with any woman. Beth Murphy got under his skin in ways he hadn't thought possible.

"Next round. If I don't get inside you I'm going to explode. I need those wet, hot walls all around me."

She closed her eyes and a flush crept across her skin. He never held back with her in bed, and it thrilled him that it turned her on rather than freaked her out or scared her off.

When she opened her eyes again, they locked on his as she shoved him back to her bed and climbed on top, straddling his waist.

Her tits jiggled, nipples hard and dark, as she lowered herself down the length of his cock, so tight he had to breathe through his nose and concentrate really hard to keep from coming right then.

Her taste was on his lips, on his tongue, tantalizing. Teasing. Seducing.

He gave in to his need to touch her. Sliding his hands up her thighs, over her belly, up her sides to those tits he loved so much. Every time he closed his eyes, it had seemed like it was Beth in his mind's eye. But the reality of her was way better than his imagination.

Bold. Full of vitality and sensuality. Sure of herself but there was vulnerability too.

Her body around his was so damned good he never wanted to leave.

He hummed his pleasure and she smiled.

"I agree with that sentiment. This is…" She stretched, arching, taking him even deeper. "So good. I have to confess that I've never considered myself a size queen. Until now."

He laughed and she writhed. Really, not that he'd say anything, but a compliment about a guy's cock? He wasn't going to complain at being called big.

She braced her hands on his belly and levered up and down, changing her angle as she pushed back to take him deeper.

Her eyes had gone glossy, her breath coming short. Her nails dug into his belly and he didn't fucking care. No. It was more—he loved it. Loved pushing her to the edge of her control. Because he was right there with her.

He rolled, looming over her, getting deeper. She pulled her knees up, wrapping her calves around him above his waist.

Her fingers tangled in his hair as she held him to her.

"The noises you make, fuck, fuck, fuck."

She made another, a strangled groan, her inner walls tightening around him.

"You're close again. Mmm, I love how easy you come."

"It's all you," she breathed out.

Her words cut off when he rolled his hips, grinding himself against her clit. Those nails of hers dug in deeper, and she bit his shoulder as she came all around him, pulling him in until there was nothing else to do but come right along with her.

She moved around in her living room in nothing more than a T-shirt and skimpy panties. Not that he was complaining. He needed to go home, and yet there he sat on her couch, watching television as his totally hot girlfriend made him tea.

Girlfriend.

Hm.

She finally settled next to him, smelling warm and sexy.

"What was going on with Clancy?"

He sighed. "Nothing."

She rolled her eyes. "It won't kill you, you know. To share your burden a little. I know something is up."

"I'm relaxed and sex tired. I don't want to talk about any of that now. I should be going, actually. I've got to be up at six."

She paused, as if to argue, but didn't press.

But he tossed and turned so much Buck got off the bed and slept on the couch. He could have shared with her. He just didn't know if he had it in him to say it all out loud.

It was Buck's little dance and his happy barks that clued Joe in to Beth's presence. She stood at the counter in the office area, and when he caught her eye, she held up a large bag.

He cleaned his hands and headed in. As usual, she looked pretty in jeans and a light sweater that hugged those spectacular tits just right. Made a man's mouth water just looking at her.

"I brought you some lunch."

Warmth coursed through him at the gesture. Being taken care of eased him, released that tangle of knots in his gut a little. "You didn't have to do that. Thank you."

She smiled, looking him over carefully. "By the looks of you this week, Joe Harris, I most assuredly do. Have you been eating at all?"

They'd put his father on a course of medication and everyone walked on eggshells hoping it would work. Hoping for some relief.

"I've been working a lot." He wanted to sit and eat with her. To take an hour. Hell, even half an hour and just listen to her voice. Let her presence work itself into his system to ease his jangled nerves.

But he was afraid of letting it go and falling apart when everyone needed him to keep it together.

"I wish I had the time to sit with you and eat. But I have a whole day's worth of work in there and not nearly enough hours to finish."

She reached up, caressing his cheek for a brief moment, and he allowed himself the weakness to lean in and take the comfort.

"That's all right. Just be sure you eat it. There's a C-O-O-K-I-E in there for your canine roommate. It's clearly marked so you don't go eating it." She looked down at Buck, who surely realized that spelling things out either meant a treat or a trip to the vet. Beth was usually the bearer of treats, so he thumped his tail hopefully.

"You wanna give it to him? He'll love you forever. Piglet that he is."

Grinning, she dug in and pulled out a cute little bag with Scottie dogs stamped all over it. She knelt and Buck put a paw on her knee. "I brought you a treat."

He barked, and she gave him one that he sucked down so fast Joe hoped he could remember doggie CPR. She laughed. "Careful there, Buck-o. Use your teeth. These will keep them all shiny too. In case you meet a cute girl dog. You want to have nice breath."

Joe looked at her, filled with emotions he warned himself not to develop where she was concerned. And he felt them anyway. She was a damned good woman.

She scratched Buck's ears and put the bag up on the counter. "For later if he's very good." She tiptoed up and kissed Joe quickly. "If you're good, I'll give you an even better treat. For now? Eat every last bit. Fried chicken and potato salad. Cornbread and some cobbler. I'd tell you I made it, but I only lie about my weight for my driver's license. Tate made it all so you know it's good. Plus it's filled with Tate love. Win/win."

He paused, bending to kiss her more thoroughly before standing straight once more. "Thank you again. For the food, for the dog treats and for thinking about me."

"Someone needs to. By the state of those circles under your eyes, you sure aren't. Why don't you come to dinner this week? Bring your parents. I *can* cook you know. Just not as awesomely as Tate. But I make a mean pan of enchiladas."

God, he could only imagine what his father might get up to at dinner at her house. He held back a barely repressed shudder.

"Busy week."

"You said that the last time I asked you to bring them to

dinner. How about we all go to the Sands?"

"I'll let you know." He held up the bag. "Gonna scarf this before I get back to work on that oil pan."

Her face fell. Just a little, but he saw it. He saw it and turned anyway, waving over his shoulder. "Talk to you soon. Thank Tate for the food too."

"See you later."

Beth grumped around the shop, peering through the racks. It had been over a week since that night when Clancy had taken Joe aside and he'd avoided talking with her about it. He'd been distracted. Dark circles under his eyes. She'd taken to showing up at the garage with lunch just so she knew he was eating.

But though it was clear he'd been touched by it, he kept distance there and it was getting to her. She couldn't even really enjoy shopping for bridesmaid dresses with Lily because of it.

Boys.

"I keep trying to act like I'm cool with it. I *should* be. I'm trying really hard to back off and let him deal with his stuff. But..."

Lily nodded. "You want him to share. Because he cares about you. Because he knows just telling you will help."

Yes. It was one thing for her to tell him it was safe to share. But his not doing it made her feel like he didn't believe it.

"It feels like he's walling me out. Which is so mean of me. Selfish. I *know* so well what it means to have family shit you just can't bear to say out loud."

"But you were a kid and whatever you dealt with, you were hostage to it. You had no escape. On the other hand, Joe is a grown man."

"It's not just that he won't talk to me about whatever is going on with his dad. He's so stressed. I know he's not getting enough rest. I invited him and his family over for dinner, and he says he's busy. Not the first time I've asked. Not the first time he's made excuses. It's beginning to feel like it's not about them, but about me. I don't like that feeling."

"If I make people wear that they'll never forgive me." Lily indicated a bridesmaid's dress Beth had in her hand.

"I was trying to get to the one behind it." She pulled the other out. "This one."

"About you how? That blue would look so gorgeous on you guys."

"Maybe I'm not meet-the-parents material. Maybe they hear the name Murphy and they can only think about my parents. God, what if they think I'm like that?"

"Whatever his hesitation is, I don't think it's that he's ashamed of you. Plus, look, Petal is a small town, but chances are, his parents either don't know who you are, or if they know about your parents, they're not stupid enough to think you'd be that way. But, if that's the case we will kick him in the face and give him dirty looks until the end of time and he will most definitely not be eating cake at my wedding. After you dump him and move on with someone way hotter, that is."

All of that was probably true. Probably. "Well it's weird and I'm getting a complex."

"Maybe you need to break it off with him. Why be with someone who makes you feel bad?" Lily indicated the dress. "Try it on."

"I don't know why I have to be the guinea pig and do this before everyone else has to."

"Because I said so. Because it's your job as the maid of honor and my best friend and because you have a fabulous sense of style. Plus it gives me a reason to look at clothes."

Lily would most likely end up making all the damned dresses for her bridesmaids anyway. "Crafty bitch."

Lily swatted her butt. "Go on. I'll be waiting."

She got into the dress in the changing room. "I don't want to break up with him. I want him to trust me enough to talk to me. Maybe I'm doing this all wrong."

Beth came out, waving a hand at the neckline. "Way too much boobage here. Tate will put someone's eye out."

Lily's laugh made her feel better. "Yeah, but yours look pretty spectacular in it. Still, we really can't have your boobs upstaging mine. *Hello*, bride here." She winked. "Maybe you can wear it to the rehearsal dinner."

"I have to wear something like this to the rehearsal dinner? It's going to be fancy? You know it's going to be wall-to-wall Murphys. We're not really fancy people."

Lily laughed and handed her several more dresses, shoving her toward the changing room again.

"My father is hosting it. He just informed me of this fact today. I haven't decided if I'm going to accept. I haven't told Nathan yet either."

Beth sighed and went back to try on the dresses. "Why shouldn't you accept? It doesn't have to mean anything. You guys are paying for this on your own. Unless you don't want any involvement with him at all." She clucked her tongue. "This one has a corset type thing at the back."

Beth went out and Lily tightened the dress's bodice. "Wow. This is definitely a contender. Since Tate is Nathan's best woman, she's going to need a different dress anyway. This one is so pretty."

"When do we get to try on your dress?"

Lily smiled. "I'm going to make it. With your help of course. It was either me making all your dresses or me making mine. I don't have the time to do both. Do you hate me?"

Beth turned, taking her friend's hands. "Why on Earth would I hate you? I can swing this dress. Tate can swing her dress. Of course I'll help in whatever way I can. You sure you want the stress? Of making it, I mean?"

"I saw this pattern at a garage sale of all places." Lily moved back to her purse and pulled it out, handing it Beth's way.

Beth looked it over, knowing immediately that the style would suit her friend beautifully. "Vintage. Perfect."

"Tea length. But it's a daytime wedding anyway. I think instead of all this lace for the sleeves I might do cashmere, as a removable bolero jacket. If the weather holds up and we have the ceremony outside, it'll be cold."

"And it'll be so soft against your skin and so pretty. Like a snow princess."

Lily nodded. "I know. Thank God you like it. It'll take some time. The skirt is pretty full, lots of pleating. But I can do it. I want to do it. It'll mean more to me. To pick out the fabric and everything."

"I'm in. Just tell me what you need and I'll do it."

"Thank you. It means more than I can say."

"I'm your best friend. You don't have to say." Beth smiled, kissing Lily's cheek.

"You're not doing it wrong. The thing with Joe I mean." Lily looked Beth up and down. "This dress is the one. The color is perfect. What do you think?"

"You don't think so? I don't know. I mean, I did game him at the beginning. I simply pushed myself into his life but I knew he dug me. But I don't want to play games. I want him to trust me. I'm…I'm falling in love with him."

Lily sucked in a breath. "Games are dumb anyway. And they never, ever work. So if you don't want to break things off, you have to give him some space and time and then figure out what you're going to do if he won't share. However," Lily continued as Beth went back into the changing room, "I think we need to strategize on how to avoid that. We're super smart, you and me. He doesn't stand a chance."

"I don't feel super smart." Beth tried on two more dresses just to be sure. "Yeah, this is the one." She got her street clothes back on and came out.

"Now, about this thing with your dad paying for the rehearsal dinner."

They waited at the register while Beth paid.

"He's…my dad. I don't want to be fighting with him. And I don't want Chris to have more negative perceptions of him. God knows there's enough damage done. He's about to be a father again. Maybe he's trying."

They headed out, down toward the fabric store a few blocks away.

"I get that. And I support you, no matter what you decide. Either way though, there's no rule saying it has to be something fancy if you don't want it. If you do, go for it. I'll wear a fancy dress and cute shoes and eat fancy food." She laughed, linking her arm through Lily's. "This is your day. Yours and Nathan's, and he's not going to give one tiny little fuck if the rehearsal dinner is swanky or not as long as you're happy."

"I'm lucky with him."

Beth laughed. "You are. He loves you. And that's really his chief motivation."

"Thanks for listening. About this whole thing. And with

Joe? I have to believe this will work out. I've seen how he is with you. He is into you in a major way. We need to be smart. And hello, that's already taken care of."

Chapter Ten

He allowed himself to get talked into going to the Tonk with William and a group of their friends. But he called Beth first.

"What are you up to tonight?"

"I'd planned on a movie with Lily and Anne. Why?"

Joe knew he sounded disappointed. But he didn't care. He hadn't really seen her in two weeks and he missed her.

"Oh. I agreed to go to the Tonk for a drink or two with William, Royal and Nathan. I thought it'd be nice if you were there too."

"Can I take that to be that you miss me?"

He liked the flirty tone in her voice. "Yeah. Like crazy. Either way, I'd like to see you tonight. Or tomorrow after I close the shop."

"Go have a drink or two. I'm meeting Lily and Anne at the theater in half an hour. I'll stop in after. You can buy me a drink and some hot wings. I might let you touch my butt while we dance. If you're lucky."

He smiled, feeling a lot less tired than he had before he'd heard her voice. Before he'd known he'd be seeing her in a few hours.

"All right. I'll see you later. Text me when you're on the way."

"See you later, Joe Harris."

He only barely registered everyone all around him at the Tonk. He'd been working a lot, and when he hadn't been, he'd been dealing with doctors and pharmacies and his parents.

Beth had shown up every day or so to bring him lunch. Or to check in. He'd been able to leave a few times to spend some time with her. Some of it had been with his lips on hers, or just walking hand in hand to the Honey Bear for a coffee.

She'd become part of his life in a way that seemed as natural as breathing. There was really no more telling himself he shouldn't want her, shouldn't feel strongly about her. He did and it was stupid to deny it.

Nathan ordered a pitcher. "Lily just texted to tell me she'd be coming by later. I have you to thank for that." He tipped his chin.

"I need to get dancing with some pretty girls if Anne is coming too." Royal poured himself a beer.

"I'm the first guy who'd say you should fight for a woman if you really want her. But, and I hate to say it because I know you're ass deep in love with my sister, but Anne may not be worth all this effort. Well, worth is not a good word. She's worth a lot of effort. But I don't know if she's ever going to get married. Even to a guy who clearly loves her." Nathan waved away a woman who indicated she wanted to dance.

William sighed. "I don't know about that, Nathan. Anne's got some messed-up ideas about marriage. But she's not a lost cause. You can't blame her. Considering the example she had growing up."

"Whatever." Royal shrugged. "I can only take it for so long. If she doesn't turn this around by the end of the year, I'm done. I love her, but I want a wife. A family. If she can't commit, if she can't admit I'm not your dad, she *is* a lost cause. I have to move on at some point."

Joe imagined giving up on Beth and he realized it filled him with fear.

"My sisters—all of them—are good women. Strong. Stronger than most any other females I've ever met. Pretty. Smart. Hardworking. All positives. But stubborn. Holy shit, stubborn." William leaned back and glowered at one of the women who'd been trying to catch Nathan's eye. "I'm about to get pissy with these women who keep trying to get you to dance. For Christ's sake, the whole town knows you're engaged to Lily."

Nathan snorted. "It's just a few of them. They know too. Not worth getting worked up over it. None of them matter one bit. If they want to keep embarrassing themselves, they should go on. Once Lily gets here, they'll back off."

"They're after Joe too." Royal laughed. "Beth will end every single one of them."

"They scatter to the wind when she comes around." Joe grinned. It was hot when she got all possessive the way she did. Not that any of the women who tried to get his attention could hold a candle to her anyway.

"I bet. Things are good with her then?" Nathan leaned in to be heard over the music.

Joe nodded. "I'm busy right now. Work and stuff. We're not getting married in a few months or anything. But we do all right."

"Since you broke the little-sister-of-your-best-friend rule, you best take care with her." William gave him a look.

Joe held his hands up. "Do you think your sister would tolerate anything else?"

William's glower softened. "I think my sister Beth has a big old soft heart, and when she cares about people, it's far easier for them to hurt her than they might think."

They'd managed to clear through a pitcher and some wings right as the women came in.

"What do you want to bet Nathan has had to beat them off with a stick tonight?" Lily said this as they weaved through the crowd toward the table.

"Doesn't matter. Also, heh, you said beat off." Anne thought this was hilarious.

Beth snickered, saying hello here and there as they made their way over. Joe had a cowboy hat on. He rarely wore one, and up until that moment, she couldn't have said it mattered to her one way or the other. But on him it *totally* worked.

When he saw her, he stood, smiling.

"Hey."

He hooked her with an arm around her waist and pulled her close, leaning down to brush his lips over hers. "Hey there."

He pulled her chair out and she sat, his arm against her shoulders. "I like the hat."

"Yeah? Your brother made me wear it."

"Which one?" She laughed.

"William."

"Ah. Well, he was right. It works on you."

"How was the movie?" He leaned close as he spoke, smelling really, really good.

"Pretty boys. Action. Lots of sweat. What's not to love?"

He stole a kiss. "Mind yourself, girl."

He took her hand, their fingers tangling.

"You're in a mood. I like it. I've missed you."

He hugged her, one armed. "Have a beer, and then you and I have some dancing to do."

"We can dance to this one while the beer is on the way out."

He stood, holding a hand out and she took it.

She'd been to the Tonk dozens of times. For a while she hated it. It wasn't their bar. They'd usually gone into Riverton because the denizens of Petal hadn't always been the friendliest to the Murphy family.

But over time, as they'd become extended family with the Chases, they'd come here more often. And as it frequently tended to happen, the Murphys took it over every time they came in. It was still full of people she didn't like. The scars of her childhood, of the torment Tate had endured, were hard to leave behind. When she saw Dolly's face, she couldn't forget the way she'd treated Beth's oldest sister.

But more than the Dollys of Petal, there were people she counted as friends.

And still? It was pretty freaking awesome to be out there on the dance floor, pulled up snug against the hottest dude in the entire place. She, Beth Murphy, had the most handsome date in the whole room. He touched her like he meant it too. It made her feel like the most beautiful person in the bar.

After the song had ended, he spun her, tucking her against his body. "Beer now."

"You're easy to please. That's a good quality in a woman."

"You're pretty good with the pleasing. Also a good quality in a man."

Lily leaned into Nathan's side, laughing at something Anne had said. The group had enlarged considerably. Shane Chase was there with his wife Cassie, Maggie and Kyle Chase were there as well.

A raucous greeting went up as they got back and seated. Lily pushed a beer her way, and Beth sure wasn't going to complain that she was extra close to Joe. This was nice. Out with her man. Out with their friends. It was comfortable and fun and really lovely.

They danced and drank beer and ate wings and nachos for hours, laughing and visiting. But with each passing hour, all she wanted was to be alone with him. To have Joe all to herself. Preferably naked.

Finally she tiptoed up as they danced, tugging on his ear to get him closer. "I think we should go back to your place. You know, Buck is probably lonely."

"Yeah?" His slow smile sent a shiver through her. "You should probably sleep over. He's missed you."

"Oh, *Buck* misses me."

He walked her back to the table to say their goodbyes but paused at her car. "I'm going to run home and grab a few things. I'll meet you at your place in about half an hour."

He kissed her quickly. "All right. Drive careful. Oh and Beth? Buck isn't the only Harris male who's missed you."

She had to force herself not to rush. It had been two weeks since they'd had anything more than stolen time. The chemistry between them was still solid, much to her relief. They'd had a few hard and fast sexual interludes, but sleeping over was different.

Waking up with him was really nice. He was big and warm, and he liked morning sex. There wasn't any *hurry-hurry-gotta-go-soon* pressure. Just hours and hours.

She grabbed a change of clothes, her toothbrush and toiletries bag and headed over to his place.

He opened up, barefoot, all well over six feet of him looking relaxed and slightly tousled.

"Man."

He paused, cocking his head. "What?"

She moved into the house. "You. You looking all hot and sexy. I like it."

Buck danced over in his adorable way, yipping, his tail wagging so hard his entire back end weaved as he moved.

She knelt, pulling a treat from her pocket. "Hello, baby." She gave it to him, bending to kiss the top of his head.

"You're spoiling him. Every time someone knocks on the door, he thinks it's you. And when it isn't, he gives me a dirty look." Joe gave her a hand up and pulled her close.

"Thanks for getting my back, Buck."

"You have on way too many clothes." He said this as he moved her toward the bedroom, all while unbuttoning her shirt.

"Police tend to look unkindly at driving around town naked."

"If I'm king, I'll change that rule."

He pulled the shirt off, not fast, but agonizingly slow. Kissing over the skin he revealed as he went. "I've missed your taste so fucking much."

She sighed happily as his lips cruised over her shoulder, across her collarbone.

He bumped her back to the bed, pulling her jeans, underpants and socks off. "Here I am, all naked in your bed. Whatever will you do to me?" She fluttered her lashes, and he laughed as he got rid of the rest of his clothes and came to join her.

"You're so beautiful." He kissed her lips, down her chin and neck. To her nipples, giving her the edge of his teeth until her breath came short.

She pushed him back. "You always go first. It's my turn."

He looked up at her, a smile on that mouth. She leaned

127

down to take it, kissing him long and slow as she skimmed her hands all over his arms and chest.

"You're a mighty big man, Joe Harris." She scooted down his body. "So much of you to touch." She licked over his ribs. "And lick."

He groaned. "Take your time. Plenty of time to lick all you want, darlin'."

She did just that. Licking down his belly, kissing up his thighs, getting him nice and worked up before she allowed herself to grab the base of his cock and angle it to lick around the head.

"I'm greedy for you." She kissed him, up the length of his cock and back down. Over and over as he gripped the bedding beneath him.

"Works for me," he managed to get out through his clenched jaw. He hissed as she sucked, hard. "Goddamn."

She smiled, looking up his body, into his eyes as he took her in.

He let her have her way with him for some time. She drove him up slowly but surely until he barely held on with his fingernails. He hadn't been with her, not like this, for two weeks, and he needed to be deep inside her. Needed that connection so much.

"Enough. You know what I want."

She pulled off. "Yeah?"

"I want that sweet, hot pussy wrapped all around my cock."

She blushed, but that didn't stop her from crawling to his nightstand to grab a condom and suit him up.

But that wasn't anything compared to what it felt like as she sank down on him.

"Jesus. Beth, you're something else, but if you move even

just a little bit, this will be over before I really get started."

She put her arms above her head, stretching like a cat. He stroked over her belly, up over her breasts.

"Gonna be hard not to move when you do that," she murmured as he tugged and rolled her nipples between his fingertips.

"You seem to like challenges."

She laughed, bending down to kiss him. He grabbed her hips and held her in place as he pressed in deep. She made a sound against his mouth, ragged, filled with desire, and he swallowed it.

He let go with one hand, moving it to her lips. She sucked his fingers inside. "Get 'em nice and wet. I'm going to use them on your clit."

She groaned as he took his fingers back, sliding them between his body and hers, finding her clit hard and ready. He stroked across that bundle of nerves, and she sucked in a breath, her inner walls tightening around him, sending a wave of pleasure rolling through his belly.

"Mmm, you're close."

She nodded as she undulated, moving her hips to take him deeper, grinding herself against his fingers at the same time.

She demanded her pleasure. There was something so amazing about that. Sexy. She wasn't ashamed of liking sex. She made it good for him, hell yes, but she expected the same. This was about the *two* of them finding pleasure together. It got him off, but also laid him bare before her. Left him vulnerable.

He loved to watch her as she approached orgasm. Loved the way her skin pinkened, the glossy look to her eyes, the way her lips parted as her breath came shorter. Her nipples darkened.

She tightened around his cock, fluttering, so hot and wet. He was right there with her and when she flew apart, he came along for the ride. Letting the waves of sensation suck him under, his hand on her hip his anchor keeping him from floating away.

He stumbled into the bathroom briefly and came back, collapsing next to her. He heard the door hinge squeak as Buck pushed in.

"Hang on, I'll shoo him out."

She put a hand on Joe's thigh. "Nah, he's okay."

Indeed, Buck had settled in his bed near the closet. Laughable since the dog normally jumped up and slept in Joe's bed.

"Good to see you use those company manners, Buck."

Buck barked and went back to chewing on his toy.

"Do you have to be at work in the morning?"

He drew lazy lines up and down her spine, unwilling to move more than that as they lay in his bed in a warm tangle.

"Not until ten. I'm done at two. Want to go for a ride in the afternoon?"

She smiled, rolling over.

"Mmm. You know how much I love that booty. But hot damn, this is my favorite side of you."

She laughed. "Good to know. I'd love to go on a ride tomorrow afternoon. Want to come over to dinner on Sunday? It's at Tate and Matt's this weekend. She's feeling a little better, but Polly Chase is making a turkey. For kicks, because she's weird. But wonderful. Like freshly baked bread."

"She sort of is. But scary. I just fixed her Lincoln last week. She's good for business."

Beth giggled. "I know I shouldn't laugh. Polly is pretty

amazing, actually. She's good at so many things. But she is the world's worst driver. It's cute how all her sons scramble to find ways to give her rides so she won't get behind the wheel. When they cart all the kids around, Edward drives the big van."

"I don't know about Sunday." He was trying to spend at least one night a week with his parents. He stopped by daily as well, but dinner was a way to keep an eye on his dad, to see how this new treatment was working. And to watch his mother too. The stress was taking a toll on her.

She shrugged. "If you decide you can make it, come over. You know it's not fancy or anything. Bring Buck with you or the kids will be sad."

Buck barked under his breath.

"Like he'd have it any other way."

"Bring your parents if you like." The hesitation in her voice tore at him.

"I'll see. If I can make it, I'll see if they can too. I can't promise, but I'll try."

She didn't say anything else.

He pulled her close, nuzzling her neck until the tension in her spine lessened. He'd talk to her about it once this treatment worked. When they were on the other side of this mess.

Chapter Eleven

"I can't believe you got me my very own helmet."

The way she smiled up at him made him warm inside.

"Well, I mean. I had an extra one. I just wanted you to have one for when we went out on a ride. We're not going to be able to do this for several months once it gets rainy and cold."

"Yes. But you made it all customized. You're adorable. Did you know that?"

"I can shoot an M16. I'm not adorable."

She laughed, clearly delighted. "You totally are." She snuggled up to him as they stood in line to get their food. "Denying it only makes you cuter. So there. Catch 22. I win. End of story."

He kissed the top of her head, keeping her close.

"I'm so hungry."

"Is that your way of telling me you aren't sharing your rings?"

She looked up at him and rolled her eyes. "Joe, who shares rings here? Get your own. I might let you have a bite of my fried peach pie. Maybe. You could get an apple one and we can share."

"Please. You're cutthroat when it comes to pie. I'm having a shake anyway."

When they got to the counter she was ready. "Chili cheese dog, rings, fried peach pie and a large tea."

The lady behind the counter approved of her proficiency with a quick nod before she looked to Joe, who gave her his order, and added a fried apple pie because he knew she'd want a bite anyway.

They settled in a table, a pile of food between them. Not much talking happened for a few minutes until she sat back with a happy sigh.

"I don't even know who invented fried pie. But God bless 'em."

"You have a pie problem." He grinned.

"I know. I should probably go to some twelve-step program. But then I'd have to give up pie. I can admit I'm powerless over it and all. That's the easy part."

"Why pie?"

"It's Tate." She paused, and he knew she was struggling with something. But in the end, Beth waved a hand. "She's magic in the kitchen. She got me hooked. But the Sands makes a pretty mean pie and cobbler too. In a pinch."

"There's a story."

She met his gaze, held it. "If you want me to share, you have to share too. That's how it works."

He sighed. "This isn't the place."

"Oh it's never the place. Or the time. I'm beginning to get tired of it. You're giving me a complex. Are you afraid you can't trust me?"

"No. It's not that. At all. I just...it's complicated and I don't want to talk about it. My dad is dealing with health problems. You're making way more out of it than it warrants."

She looked him over, clearly disappointed. And truth be

told, he was pretty disappointed in himself for ducking her question. But he had so little time that was free of the mess with his father. Was it so wrong to want to keep that out while he had Beth all to himself?

The rest of their lunch went fine. She teased him here and there. Held on as they rode back to Petal. But there was a distance between them. Of his own design. Once it was there, he realized just how much she'd worked to fill it before.

The sun was setting by the time they rolled back into town. He pulled up at her place.

"Want to come in? There are some good movies on cable. I was going to watch one and eat popcorn. You can even go get your son to bring him over. I noticed he liked popcorn."

He snorted a laugh. "That dog loves everything. Popcorn. Carpet lint. Whatever." He paused. "Yeah. I'll be back in a few."

"You can spend the night if you like."

"I've got to be at the shop early."

She shrugged. "Okay. See you in a few minutes." She turned and went inside.

Beth called in the shampoo and color order and tapped her pen.

"Stop that tapping. I'm going to get a tic in my eye," Tate called out. "Come out here and tell me what the hell is going on."

"I'm working."

"You are not. Come out here. I have brownies."

Well, why didn't she say that up front?

"All I'm gonna say is if you lead with that, people will be far quicker to comply with your imperious demands." She put a mug of hot water with a teabag in it at Tate's station.

"Hello, Beth." Polly Chase reached out to squeeze Beth's hand.

"Afternoon, Mrs. Chase." She smiled at Polly and then looked back to Tate. "Brownies?"

Polly laughed.

"Over there. Cookies too. Figured you might want some extra to take over to Joe."

"Joe can get his own cookies." Beth shoved half a brownie in her mouth and let the chocolate soothe her annoyance. "The man is going to make me gain fifteen pounds from annoyance eating."

"Ah, so the pen tapping is about a man." Polly sighed. "They can be so infuriating. But they're also cute and handy and they can reach high shelves and they pump your gas so your hands don't get smelly."

Beth laughed. "Sure. And they put out a lot of heat so you use less electricity to keep warm. And they look nice in jeans. They say sweet things, especially if they think they might get lucky."

"What has Joe done to make you cranky then, sweetie pie?"

Polly Chase had a way about her. Soothing in a very no-nonsense way. She was a lot like a mother to Tate, and when Tate had come into the Chase family, Polly had not only taken in Tate, but all the Murphy kids. She was normal. She and her husband had a loving, thriving marriage and a healthy family. No one got drunk and hit anyone. No one called anyone fat or stupid. Her advice meant something.

She sat, watching Tate backcomb and spray Polly's long hair up into her signature style. Helmet hair, as Anne called it.

But it worked on Polly, as most things did. Beth figured it was because nothing, not even a hairdo, dared not to work on Polly Chase.

"He's nice to me. Respectful. He never even looks at other women. Well, he's good at making me think so, which is fine. He makes me laugh. I love his dog. He makes me feel beautiful. But he has a wall up." She shared a little about the situation with his family and how Joe froze up any time she invited them anywhere or asked about them.

"I've heard things around town about Carl." Polly folded her hands in her lap. "Erratic behavior. He's been banned from a few places. That's got to be rough on Joe. Sometimes you have to be patient. Other times though? Well, other times you have to push a little. Only you can know when and if it's that time."

"Maybe he's ashamed. Maybe Carl has a drinking problem. Or drugs." Tate kept working as she spoke.

"I don't know. I could poke around. People know he and I are together. They come up to me all the time and try to talk about it. I don't want to hear it. I don't gossip like that."

Polly smiled then.

"Mrs. Chase, you're scary when you smile like that."

"She's sneaky." Tate squeezed Polly's shoulder.

"It's a good smile. You surely do care about him to protect him like that. Gossip can be fun. But it can also be mean and come from a bad place. You're smart to keep that away from yourself. For what it's worth? I think Joe Harris is a good boy. He talked about you nonstop when I was in for repairs last week. And the time before that. I've never heard you talk about anyone like this. I like that. I know he's come to dinner a few times at Tate and Matt's. Why don't you ask him to come to our house this Sunday?"

"I invited him last weekend and he ducked it. Well, I invited him and his parents. I've asked them over for dinner more than once. I've asked them out to dinner. I considered just going over or calling his mother myself, but that's way too meddlesome. I don't want to go around him."

"You want him to want it on his own."

"Yes. Anyway, we have a date tonight. Dinner after work at the Sands. I'll ask him then. Maybe I'll just stop asking his parents. It seems petty. Am I being petty?"

"You're not being petty. You love him. It's written all over you. You want him to be as invested in you as you are in him. That includes family. Just stick with it. He loves you too." Tate leaned over to kiss Beth's cheek. "I know a few things. Trust me."

"I do trust you. But you're pregnant and you're sort of crazy when you're knocked up." Beth grinned at her sister, who stood at least half a foot shorter. She was already showing at the halfway mark.

Polly laughed happily as she took herself in, patting her hair. "I do love that you never try to talk me into anything else. You do my hair perfectly."

"It suits you. Though if you ever want to go wild and do red and a shorter bob? I'd love that too. What matters most about hair, is that you love it. It makes you happy. And that's all I care about."

Beth watched the two and ached a little. What if Joe's mom and Beth could be like this? Teasingly close? She didn't know his parents very well. Just sort of in passing. His mother seemed lovely. A little shy, but lovely.

Polly took her hand. "What does your heart say? You've got a good head on your shoulders. You're not one to let yourself get walked all over just for a pretty face. What does your heart tell you about Joe?"

"That he's worth it." Her voice cracked, but she cleared her throat and Tate grabbed a tissue.

"So fight for him."

She took her time with her appearance. What? She was supposed to lie to herself? Of all people? Puhleeze. She wanted him to know just what he had, inside and out. She wasn't her mother; she didn't solely rely on her looks to fill all her empty spots. Looks were only on the outside anyway.

But she was a pretty woman. She knew it. She knew her strengths, and there was no harm in working them to ten so Joe Harris's eyes popped out when he saw her walk through the front doors of the Sands.

Beth had given him her heart. She showed him how much she cared about him in every way she could. But there was absolutely no harm in some glossy red lips and a snug bright blue sweater to go with her blue jeans too. She tousled her hair, which Tate had given big, loose curls to. She looked hot. Ha! And her underwear matched.

She would fight for him, damn it. Polly and Tate had been right. Anything worth having took work. He was worth it. She would use every single thing she had in her arsenal to let him know not only what he had in her, but that she understood what she had in him.

She tucked her overnight bag and some treats for Buck into her trunk and headed out.

Joe had been listening to some story Nathan had been relating. What he noticed first was the way Royal and Jacob's roommate Trey looked up, openmouthed.

He turned and saw why immediately. Beth had come in looking so fucking gorgeous and sexy their booth wasn't the only one staring. She was a pretty woman, but her pretty had been turned up straight to luscious. Her hair was big in the way a Southern man could appreciate. Her makeup accentuated her beauty, her eyes looked smoky, her lips red and plump. And that sweater.

"Stop staring," he told Royal and Trey.

"That's my sister." Jacob, the youngest Murphy, whacked his friend.

"Your sister is freaking gorgeous."

"And taken." Joe stood and moved to her. She gave him a smile, one she never gave anyone else.

"Hello there, long, tall and handsome."

He pulled her close. "Hello yourself. You're going to cause an accident or something. Darlin', you're looking mighty fine tonight. I don't want to be here at all. I want you all to myself."

Her eyes shone with amusement. "I have on a new bra and panty set. Same color as the sweater."

"Damn. You're going to kill me."

She laughed. "I'm all yours, Joe Harris. Don't break me. Or my heart."

The laugh died away as he realized the enormity of the moment, but before he could respond, everyone at the table called out their greetings, and he groaned, turning her to head over.

Lily gave Beth a raised brow and Beth shrugged.

"Hey all."

Everyone greeted her as she got settled, snuggled into his side.

Lauren Dane

"I saw Polly today. She said she'd been showing up at your house to try and finagle a look at the dress."

Lily laughed. "She has! She's got great excuses and has taken to bringing baked goods to bribe me. But I keep telling her I won't fit into the dress if I ate all the stuff she brought."

"She's a menace with all the baked goods. With Tate on one side, baking even more than usual because she's pregnant, and Polly on the other, my jeans are all getting tight."

Nathan shook his head. "Not really a chore to have women bake stuff for me though."

Joe looked down at Beth. "Or to have a girlfriend with a connection to the font of baked goods."

"Girlfriend?" Royal whistled. "Just watch out. Murphy women. Good Lord."

Nathan thought that was hilarious.

"The one I have is pretty perfect." Joe took her hand, accepting that she was real and his and maybe he should stop holding back.

"This is very true." Lily gave him a look that said if he forgot it, he'd be sorry in more than one way.

Beth looked over the specials menu and hummed her delight. "Smothered pork chop night. Awesome."

"Tate's are better."

"We're not at Tate's, Nathan." Beth said it automatically, not even looking up. Joe liked the easy back and forth between Beth and her brother.

"You missed a really good dinner Sunday." Nathan looked over to Joe. "Turkey, ham, macaroni and cheese, three different kinds of potatoes. Fresh bread. It was insane."

He'd been with his parents. It hadn't been a bad night, but there was the sense of watching and waiting. His father had
140

been pretty quiet. No outbursts, but he'd had an air of sadness Joe couldn't seem to get around.

"I'm gonna pop Dolly in the face if she doesn't stop sending you looks."

Joe had been busily pretending he wasn't staring at Beth's boobs. He started when she spoke. "What, darlin'?"

She laughed, looking up at him after she'd ordered her food.

"I said, I was going to punch Dolly for sending you all those come-hither looks."

Truth be told Dolly had been relentlessly pursuing him. She showed up at the shop all the time. Buck growled at her, which Joe thought showed the dog's good taste. Clearly, because he danced with joy every time he caught sight of Beth. He'd told Dolly many times that he wasn't interested, that he was seeing Beth and to back off.

"There's a thing between her and the Murphys." Lily snorted, shooting Nathan a look.

Nathan put his hands up in surrender. "Why you looking at me like that? I never dated her."

Lily snorted. "No, you were engaged to her bestie though. And Dolly and her cabal went after Tate for a while. She's a nasty piece of work and it is no surprise she's alone."

Beth snickered. "A spinster."

Lily started laughing. "All alone. Watching episodes of Hoarders and eating TV dinners. Maybe she'll order up a Russian groom."

"Great idea. One that doesn't speak any English so he won't know how full of it she is."

Joe grinned, shaking his head as they kept on.

"Best to just stay out of their way when they get like this."

Nathan sipped his tea.

"I have zero interest in Dolly. Just sayin'."

Beth looked his way. "Course you don't. You have me. But she needs to keep her mitts and her eyes to herself. Sheesh." She went back to laughing with Lily.

"Guess she told you." Trey grinned.

"My sisters don't mess around." Jacob chuckled.

Royal heaved a sigh. "No kidding."

"Man comes to a point in his life when that's what he needs and he's not too proud to admit it. I like a feisty woman." Joe grinned.

"Ha. Good thing since this family doesn't seem to make any other kind." Nathan winked at Beth.

"Jacob, I bumped into Heather yesterday." Beth turned her attention to her baby brother. "She didn't know you'd moved back to Petal."

"Heather is engaged. My living situation isn't her concern."

"Well, now. There's a story here. Do tell." Joe waggled his brows.

"Jacob and Heather were inseparable in high school," Beth explained.

"And then I went to college. And she moved on. She's going to marry someone else."

Beth shrugged. "She sure seemed interested."

"Leave it be, Beth. How'd you feel if Steffie's friends were plotting to break up Nathan's engagement?"

Stefanie was Nathan's ex. A sort of crazy woman who'd apparently taken it upon herself to announce their engagement without telling Nathan. And then she'd capped it by showing up at Nathan's place with wedding invitations.

Beth rolled her eyes. "First of all, Steffie is a dingus. However, I didn't give Heather a key to your apartment and tell her to get in your bed naked. She came in for a haircut. We chatted. *She* asked after you. I told her you and Trey had a place here in town and that you were splitting your time between Joe's shop and Tim's plumbing business. That's hardly plotting—"

A loud crash interrupted the good-natured teasing, grabbing the attention of just about everyone in the place.

Murmurs began to get louder as everyone turned toward the side doors leading out to the other end of the street, right off the alley.

"What on Earth is going on?"

"It's Friday night. Probably some spillover from Buck a Bud night at the Pumphouse." Nathan shrugged.

The yelling got more distinct, and Beth turned to Joe as it hit him just who it was.

"You're part of it! Get the hell out of my way or I'll make you."

Joe's stomach dropped as he stood. He put a restraining hand on Beth's shoulder. "Stay here." He rushed toward the sounds of the fray. Voices rising. More voices joining in.

Beth followed. He turned. "I said stay back. He's not in his right mind and I don't want you hurt."

She took his hand. "Be quiet. Go deal with him."

"I mean it, Beth. Back off." He took his hand back and jogged over, leaving her in his wake.

His dad stood in the alley swinging a lead pipe, screaming at one of the cooks. His hair stuck up in patches. His eyes were wild, leaving behind any hope of calm any time soon. His clothes were disheveled and his left forearm had a cut that was bleeding pretty heavily.

"Carl, calm down," the cook reasoned. "There ain't no need for this. Someone's gonna call the cops."

"Go on ahead and call 'em. Don't think I don't know what you're up to!" He moved in with that pipe, swinging it at the cook's head.

Joe stepped between them, grabbing the pipe and yanking. His father stumbled back as he lost his grip and then he rushed Joe, head down, straight into his belly.

They burst into the restaurant as people dived from the way. The moment was eerily similar to some of the experiences he'd had in Iraq, and his world, the then and the now, shifted slightly, sending him off balance in more ways than one.

But he didn't have time for any of it. He had to deal with this before it got any worse.

Nathan and Royal approached, ready to help. Joe couldn't think about where Beth was or what she thought. His father was already bleeding. Joe had no idea if he was injured in any other way.

Carl went sprawling backward as Joe was able to get his feet, to stop the movement of his dad's attack.

People tried to help, but it only made things worse as his father's panic seemed to grow and grow.

The yelling, punctuated by a scream here and there made Joe's head hurt.

"Dad. Stop." He kept his voice calm, his hands open. Trying to get his father to focus on him, to see it was all right to let go of this rage.

Then sirens sounded in the background, and his father's eyes glazed again as he lunged, trying to punch someone nearby. Joe grabbed the back of his dad's shirt to haul him away. Calm-talk time was gone.

"Stop it! Dad! You're out of control."

"Can't you see? They're all in on it. Are you too? Hell, maybe *she* is."

His dad had indicated Beth as he wriggled from Joe's grasp, rushing toward her.

Not Beth, damn it.

"No!" Time slowed as Joe moved to tackle him as several others did, which sent their balance out of whack and his dad kept going, right through one of the big windows, which shattered as Joe went through right with him, trying to protect his dad the best he could.

Two cops had arrived, one of them was Shane Chase, who helped Joe to his feet.

"What the hell? You okay?" Shane looked him over.

More sirens, and Joe hoped one of them was an ambulance because his father was bleeding profusely.

Beth rushed up, holding towels.

"Stay back, Beth!" Shane ordered. "Honey, there's glass all over the place."

"I'm aware. At least get these on Mr. Harris to stanch the bleeding." Her voice was strangely calm. Her manner was matter-of-fact.

Joe didn't want to look at her. Shame filled him. Warring with frustration, anger and exhaustion.

"Joe is bleeding too."

"There's an ambulance here now. They've got it." Thankfully Shane kept her away. "Joe, you gotta get back. I need to get your dad in some cuffs. I'm sorry."

"He's having mental problems. He...he's been on a new

treatment. I guess it's not working." He scrubbed his hands over his face, jerking back when he realized he had tiny shards of glass all over his skin.

"Arrest me if you have to." Beth shoved her way over. She thrust a wet hand towel at Joe. "Let me get your face cleaned up."

She was everything that had been good in his life. Everything right and healthy and this...*this* thing with his father had gone and fucked it up.

He'd taken his attention away from his dad and put it toward Beth, and now he had to make a choice. The last thing she needed was for this mess to spill into her life. He couldn't bear to look at her.

"Just leave me be, for God's sake."

She stepped back, and he made the mistake of glancing up, finding her bloody. But she appeared to be fine enough to narrow her eyes at him. "You're bleeding. He's not going anywhere but the hospital. You can take thirty seconds to stop that blood from getting into your eye."

"Look, Beth." He gazed around at the chaos. They had loaded his father onto a gurney and were cleaning him up and strapping him down. Joe lowered his voice. "I'm sorry, but this thing isn't going to work."

"What thing?" She moved closer, reaching up to brush his hair from his face but he stepped back. If she touched him he'd lose all his resolve.

"This thing. The you-and-me thing. Beth, I like you. But my life is a thousand kinds of fucked up right now. I don't have the time or the energy to have a relationship of any kind."

"You're *dumping* me?"

"You can ride to the hospital with him if you like." The

paramedic tapped Joe's shoulder.

Beth waved him on. "Go. I'll check on you later."

"Don't. Beth, it's over." He turned his back on her and got into the back of the ambulance, careful not to look at her again.

Chapter Twelve

"*Over* my ass." Beth watched as the ambulance pulled away.

"Honey, come away from all that glass." Nathan put an arm around her, steering her from the mess.

A dude covered in blood had just dumped her.

Lily, eyes wide, took Beth's hands, rubbing them between her own. "Sweetie, your hands are ice cold and you've got blood on you too. You were really close to the window when it broke. You've got bits of glass everywhere. Come on. Let's get you home so you can clean up."

She pulled away. "No."

Nathan got that look around his mouth that said he was going to be stern. It usually made her feel better. Or at the very least, well enough to poke at him. But that's not what she needed.

"Did you get hurt? You're bleeding. Let us help." He stepped closer.

Not physically. Nothing on the outside hurt.

"I need to be alone."

Lily looked between them. "Honey?"

"I need to be by myself." She started to walk away and Lily caught up.

"What the hell is going on?"

"He dumped me. I—" Tears began to well up and she couldn't afford them just then.

"Let me help you. Please. I hate seeing you like this. He didn't mean it. You know he didn't."

"What's happening?" Jacob called out.

"I can't with this right now. Please. Let me be."

Lily's eyes were full of emotion. She reached toward Beth. "There's no way your brothers are going to let you just walk off in the dark after that scene. You know them."

"I need to be alone!" She yelled it and then instantly felt awful. "I'm sorry."

Lily's bottom lip wobbled as she gave Beth a hug. "*I'm* sorry. I just want to make it better. Go. I'll hold them off. You better pick up when I call you in an hour. You get an hour, Beth, and then your best friend is declaring make-it-better rights. Don't make me come find you."

She kissed Lily's cheek and took off, glad she'd worn her flat boots that night.

Tate heard the knock on the door. "I'll get it," she called out to Matt, who was in the bathroom with the girls, monitoring their bath time.

She opened and nearly had a heart attack at the sight of Beth, weeping and covered in blood. "Good Lord!" She grabbed Beth, pulling her into the house and slamming the door in her wake, locking it. "What is it? Are you all right? Is there someone after you?"

Beth shook her head, speechless but for the crying.

Matt ran out, holding a soaking-wet baby. "What's going
149

on?"

Beth's attention jerked to where he stood with the baby. "Oh God, I'm so sorry. I just didn't know where else to go." Beth kept crying, which alarmed Tate more than she wanted to say. Beth didn't even cry when she was a baby. Their father had reacted to it with rage, even as babies they'd known to keep quiet to avoid his notice.

"There's blood all over you." Matt handed Lil Beth to Tate, who tucked the towel around her better so she wouldn't get cold. He kept his voice level and calm. "Honey, let me see what's wrong."

Matt was trained as a paramedic, he'd make it better. Tate held Lil Beth as she tried to squirm out of her arms to get to her aunt.

Beth's face, so pale, contrasted against the blood, showed pain and it made Tate's stomach hurt.

"It's not me. It's not my outside that's hurt."

That brought tears to Tate's eyes.

Matt moved slowly, so Beth could see exactly where he was going and what he was doing. He brushed her hair back away from her forehead. "I can see glass in a few places. Come into the kitchen with me. I've got a first aid kit in there. Tate, why don't you call Shane?"

"No!" Beth grabbed Matt's arm. "It's...they were already involved. Please."

Matt sighed but since Beth allowed him to lead her into the kitchen, he didn't say anything else.

Tate looked to Beth after shaking her head sharply at Matt. "I'll be right back. I want to get Meg dried off and both girls dressed."

"I'm sorry. I shouldn't have come. I don't want to scare the girls."

"Hush about that. They love you to pieces. This is going to sting a little." Matt worked steadily, pulling glass out of her skin and cleaning up after that.

She looked off into the middle distance, knowing he was torn between his job and his responsibility to her as family. She needed to explain enough to make him feel better. "Joe's dad went through the front window of the Sands. He rushed at me. Joe knocked him aside to protect me and they both went out the window."

"Jesus."

"He was crazy. I mean like really crazy. He came in starting fights with everyone in sight. Joe and one of the cooks tried to calm him down. And then the window. The cops came. An ambulance came and took Joe's dad to the hospital. Joe went with him. I just...I shouldn't have come. I'm sorry."

Matt tipped her chin up, kissing the tip of her nose. "I said no more of that. Where else would you go but to Tate? Hmm? She's your momma as sure as she's Meg and Beth's momma. You're family, sweetheart. Of course you should have come."

Matt washed his hands. "I'm going to go get the girls down. Tate will be out in a minute. You're welcome here any time. Do you understand?"

She nodded, very close to crying again.

Tate came into the kitchen. "First, why don't you take a shower? You have clothes here. Change into some sweats and warm socks and then you can have some whiskey with a tiny bit of tea and I can have some hot milk. Then you'll tell me."

Beth wanted to hug her, but she wasn't sure if there was any glass left. So she obeyed, taking the clothes Tate had brought with her and then shuffled into the bathroom, closing the door in her wake.

She turned the water on and stood there, letting the tears go, letting herself cry as hard as she could. Because once those were gone, she needed to get herself back together somehow.

But it was safe here to let it go. So as she shampooed her hair, making sure there was no glass, as she got rid of her fabulous makeup job, as she washed the millions of cuts she'd gotten and hadn't even known it as the window had shattered and the glass had flown, she allowed herself to fall apart.

Tate would help her put her pieces back together when she was ready.

And knowing that helped.

Tate looked up as Matt came back into the room after he'd put the girls down to sleep. He'd have called his brother as well, she knew.

He waved her to sit. "Going to start the tea and warm milk. You should get off your feet."

She smiled his way. "I'm fine. The nausea is nearly all gone. I can heat water and milk, you know."

He stalked over, kissed her and gently but firmly sat her down. "I'll tell you what I know if you rest."

"You fight dirty for such a pretty man."

"How else can I manage my wife?" He winked. "Beth said Joe's dad went crazy at the Sands and that he rushed her. Joe ran him down to keep him from harming her and they both went out the big front window."

"Holy fuck." Whoops, her fuck problem tended to come out when she was really upset. Thank goodness the girls were down. "Sorry. What did Shane say?"

Matt put a kettle on to get some water hot and poured milk

into a saucepan for her. Her gorgeous man, so protective. He'd always been there when she needed him. Always. A fabulous father, a wonderful husband. It was still hard to believe he was hers. Man, she was lucky.

"I've heard you say lots filthier than fuck, Venus." He winked at her and went back to the telling. "Shane's glad she's here. I guess she left the scene, and Nathan and Jacob were pissed and worried about her. Lily said she needed to be left alone. She'll need to talk to the cops though. But it can wait for now. Carl is under observation and being treated for multiple wounds. I'm gonna say stitches most likely, probably watching for signs of a concussion, that sort of thing. You know Shane's got to be careful how much he says about anything hospital related. Anyway, he says Carl was pretty messed up. Joe was treated for lacerations. He's got some bruised ribs, but nothing is broken. He's still at the hospital with his mom."

Tate blew out a breath. "Well, I'm glad they're all okay. But Beth is my main concern. I've never seen her like this." She got up, wiping the counter down just to do something with her hands to keep them from shaking so much. "A control freak, my baby sister. Especially of her emotions. She broke her arm when she was four. Oh fuck that, our father broke her arm. Goddamned piece of shit. She didn't cry. She just tucked in between me and William, and she held on, even when they were setting it. So stoic."

Matt moved to her, wrapping his arms around her shoulders. "Venus, you undo me." He kissed each eyelid. "I love you so much. She came here to you. Tucking up into you just like she did then. She'll be all right. She's a strong woman, like her older sister."

"I hate it when she's upset. She's a good woman, Matthew. What did that man do to her?"

"He dumped me." Beth came down the hall, keeping her voice low. "I hope you don't mind but I checked on the girls and gave them night-night kisses."

Tate loved her sister so much. "They'd have been mad if you hadn't."

"Meg said she wasn't going to sleep until you came in anyway." Matt put the tea and milk out on the coffee table. "Call me if you need me." He hugged Beth. "We'll get this set to rights. I've never met the man who can resist a Murphy sister."

Beth gave him a smile—not a big one—but it reached her eyes and that was a step in the right direction.

Tate kissed him. "Thank you."

"Any time, Venus. I put out pillows and blankets. Do not drive her home yourself if she wants to go home. I'll do it. I have tomorrow off and I don't want you out so late." He took her chin, looking into her eyes. "Okay? Please?"

"She promises. Though I can walk home. It's not that far."

He looked around Tate to Beth. "Except no. Jeez, ladies, let me do stuff sometimes, okay? Stay over. Tate's making waffles and the girls would love to have you. I'm sure they'd even let you watch *Mary Poppins* a few times. But if you want to go home, come get me. I'm just catching up on all the stuff on the DVR that Tate hates anyway."

Beth nodded. "All right. Thank you, Matt."

Beth sat back, tucking her feet beneath her and turning her body toward Tate.

"Take it slow, Matt had a pretty liberal hand with the whiskey in the tea."

Beth sipped and agreed. But the warmth felt good. The burn took away some of the fear, eased the panic.

"Baby, this is killing me. Tell me so I can fix it." Tate took her hand and Beth put her head on her sister's shoulder.

"I guess I know what he's been skirting all these months. He dumped me."

"I don't understand. He broke up with you? You had a date, right?"

"Right on the sidewalk outside the Sands. Covered in blood, a bruise coming up on his cheek. He was so..." Beth closed her eyes as she remembered it all over again. "He was in so much pain. Not physical pain. He was heartsick. And ashamed."

"Start at the beginning."

"It was good. The date I mean. Jacob and Trey were there. Nathan and Lily. Royal. Joe. He was affectionate. He said I was his girlfriend. We'd gotten to a new level. I know we did. And then there was all this yelling and Joe got up because it was his dad and then everything happened so fast. It was so loud and people kept trying to help and he was trying to calm his dad down and it was crazy. I was standing on the booth. The one we were all sitting at. I was watching it all unfold and then his dad looked to me and started screaming about how I was part of it. Whatever *it* was. And then he rushed at me. I didn't have time to react. Nathan grabbed the back of my sweater. I think he climbed up behind, in the booth behind ours. And then Joe rushed his dad, like to tackle him. And they both sailed right through the glass and I tipped out too. I didn't get cut too bad. I think Nathan's grabbing me helped. And Joe of course."

Beth sipped the tea and tried to calm down. She closed her eyes, but saw it all again.

"Joe wrapped himself around his dad. Even after all that craziness, he tried to protect his father as they went through the window. So there was all this noise and mess and the cops had arrived and Roni handed me a bunch of wet towels to stanch all the bleeding. Joe was so lost. Watching his dad as they tried to treat him. They strapped him down to the gurney and I tried to help him. Joe, I mean. He had a big slice above his eye and it was bleeding pretty bad. But he pushed my hands away and then he broke up with me. Right there. In front of God and everyone he dumped me."

Tate let out a long breath. "He doesn't mean it."

"That's the thing. At first it hurt so bad. Like he blamed me. But then I realized that wasn't it. He said some crap about how he had too much to do and didn't have time for a relationship. But his whole life can't be about his father. He came back here to help them. He's a good man, Tate. He needs someone to help him. He loves me, Tate. I know it. I *know* it. And I love him. He needs help and I'm going to give it to him."

Tate smiled. "There she is. My girl. You have a plan."

"I yelled at Lily. In the middle of the sidewalk. I need to call her. She took on Nate and Jacob to give me some time to get away. I came here. I just needed you."

Tate put her milk down to wrap her arms around Beth. "Of course you do. And I'm here. Because I love you. Now, what are you going to do?"

"It wasn't alcohol. Though he was drunk. He's not right. Joe mentioned his dad being on a new round of treatment so I'm guessing it's mental illness of some kind. So I'm going to research. Get as much information as I can. He needs an advocate so I'm going to be one. Trey's sister is a mental-health nurse. I'll ask him for her number." Making plans made the problem seem far less insurmountable. It was how she made it through. Step by step.

She felt better already.

"Matt called Shane. Joe was treated for lacerations and released. He's at the hospital with his mother. Carl is still there, under observation. Shane didn't say much about that. You know he already said more than he should have."

"Probably some sort of mental-health hold. Better there than jail. I wish I could go over there. Just to be with him. But I don't know his mom very well, and I don't want to be more hindrance than help. I need to know what to do."

"I'll get you a pad and a pen and the laptop. You can call Trey after you check in with Lily. Nathan will be going crazy with worry."

She hugged her sister tight. "Thank you."

"For what?" Tate had no idea how much she meant to them. It was part of how wondrous she was.

"For being here when I needed you. For knowing what I needed to do and for making it happen."

"How many times have you been there for me? To pick up the pieces when I fell apart? I love you. It breaks my heart to see you upset. But *this* Beth I can deal with much easier than the one who was in tears. You want him. He needs you. We'll make it happen. Heck, if he gets too out of line, we'll get Polly involved."

Beth laughed. "He'd never know what hit him."

"For now, let's keep it between us." Tate winked as she got up. "Call Lily before Nathan shows up. Or worse, William hears about it."

"I don't know why you couldn't just say all this at the Sands. I could have given you a ride to Tate's. You ran off in the dark. After you'd nearly been thrown through a window."

"I'm sorry, Nathan." And she really was. She could see in his mannerisms that he'd been worried. "I needed to get away. I was..."

Tate rolled her eyes and handed her brother a cookie. "She was weeping."

Nathan's mouth dropped open and Beth felt even worse at the look on his face. "I'm going to punch Joe Harris in the face."

"No. It's not his fault. He thinks he's protecting me. He's embarrassed."

Nathan hugged her. "He made you cry. You never cry."

"I love him."

Nathan sighed heavily. "All right. I know you well enough to understand what that means. What can I do to help?"

Lily squeezed Beth's hand before she kissed Nathan quickly. "I love you. You big marshmallow."

"Lily, she never cries. Not even when—" He shut up quickly.

Beth shook her head, taking his hand. "No more silence. That's part of the problem. If I cried, he won. Our father I mean. So no matter what, I wouldn't let him make me cry. I could control that. I never wanted to give in to him. To give him the satisfaction. Not even when he broke my arm. Not even when he punched me so hard he knocked out my tooth. I won't ever let him make me cry. But that's not my shame to own, and Joe needs to understand he can't own shame for anything other people do."

"I've been your best friend since we were kids and you never told me? My God. Beth." Lily looked to them all, shaking her head. "It's a miracle, you know. That you all turned out to be so wonderful and loving."

"We did it to spite them both. Now, Trey gave me his sister's number. She gets off shift in an hour. I'm going home. Don't worry, I'll be back for waffles in the morning. I want to see my girls. But I have stuff to do between now and then, and I don't want to wake them up. Nathan is going to drop me home. Go snuggle with your wife."

Matt kissed her cheek. "We'll see you tomorrow morning then. Don't make me come get you."

Joe had just crawled back home when he heard a knock on his door. He ignored it, but it kept on.

He opened up, saw it was Beth and had to fight the need to simply hold her.

He had to satisfy himself by asking after her. "You all right?"

She touched the butterfly bandage on her forehead. "Just a few cuts. Nothing major. What about you?"

"Fine. Look, Beth, we said all there was to say last night. I'm exhausted. I need to sleep before I go to work a while."

"You're not going to work. You have people to help you. Accept that help and get some rest. Jacob told me the garage was fully staffed for the rest of the weekend without you. I'll take Buck for the day. Just get some sleep and come get him when you're ready."

He sighed, wanting her so bad his skin itched. Buck didn't do his usual dance at the sight of her, he was too linked with Joe's emotional mood to do that. But he did come over, tail wagging.

"We're broken up. I can handle my fucking dog."

She narrowed her eyes at him for a moment. "I'm sure you can. Don't use the F word around him. He's sensitive. Call me when you're ready. I've got a bowl and stuff at my place." She looked to Buck. "Come on then, Mr. Buck. We're having a play date."

And then she stole his dog!

He watched her go, watched her get Buck into her car and go around to the driver's side. She turned back to him. "I'm not going anywhere far." She meant with the dog, but he knew she meant in general too. And though he couldn't afford to be comforted by it. He was anyway. "Get some sleep. You know where to find me when you're ready."

He went back inside and stood, back against the door for so long he just slid down and sat, staring into nothingness.

Christ. He should be angry with her for dealing with his staff. But he couldn't be. All he could do was remember the way her face fell when he'd broken up with her. And yet, she'd been there, offering to take Buck so he could sleep without noise and distractions.

He looked at his hands. Abrasions on his knuckles. Middle finger splinted. He'd taken his mother home after sitting at her side all night long. His father had been heavily sedated so at least his yelling had stopped.

His mother seemed totally deflated. She was cried out. Had wrung her hands and blamed herself a thousand times. She'd been watching him that night. His dad was supposed to have been watching the game. She'd left the room and when she returned with snacks, he was gone.

She'd gone glassy eyed. Leaning on Joe to make the decisions and choices. She'd lost hope and he didn't blame her. The hope they'd felt as his father had assented to the treatment had been so wonderful after all the worry and upset. The bitterness that it not only hadn't worked, but the spectacular, public failure lay on his tongue, in his heart.

His mother was a simple woman. Not stupid. Certainly not naïve. But simple. She came from a world where if you were sick you took a pill and got better. Right then he didn't know what was next. He didn't even have the strength to imagine it just yet.

With a heavy sigh, he made himself stand. He needed a shower and at least four hours' sleep. First though, he needed to check in with his staff. He believed Beth and he trusted Jacob, but it was his business after all.

Chapter Thirteen

Joe ended up sleeping seven hours. Like a stone. What had eventually woken him up was a call from his sister, checking in and mightily apologetic for waking him up.

He filled her in with what he knew. Which wasn't a lot. Dissuaded her from coming down. There was nothing she could do, and it didn't seem to him like it would help to disrupt the kids' school and activity schedule. Not then in any case.

He called the hospital to check in. He wouldn't be allowed in to see his dad, even if he'd wanted visitors. His mother was staying with her sister in Riverton, which filled Joe with a sense of guilty relief. One less thing to be responsible for.

He shuffled into his kitchen, realizing his pantry was empty. He'd order a pizza or something. But first he needed to collect Buck.

He tried not to look closely at his phone, with Beth's picture smiling up at him. He needed to delete that, but he didn't want to right then.

She answered, laughing, Buck yipping in the background. "Why aren't you resting?"

"I slept seven hours. I'm good. I can come get Buck. I've got to get groceries anyway."

"I'll bring him over in twenty minutes." She hung up.

He didn't want her in his apartment. He wanted a big moat around his life to keep her out. It was too hard otherwise.

But she was stubborn. He smiled, even though it wasn't wise. He was too tired not to.

He opened to her knock and Buck barked up at him once as he came inside.

"Thank you. For taking him today."

She breezed past where he'd been attempting to block her from coming inside. She headed into the kitchen where she put the bags she'd been holding up on the counter.

"Beth..."

"Be quiet. I'm making you some food."

"You need to leave. Damn it. We're not together anymore. I don't need you to make me food. I can cook."

She sighed, moved to him, led him to a chair at the table and pushed him into it. "You. Sit. I'm going to make you a meal and you're going to appreciate it. You will not tell me you broke up with me. I was there."

He frowned, but she simply ignored him and went back to work.

"My father is an alcoholic." She said this matter of fact as she began to get out pots and pans. "I never really realized other people's dads weren't like mine until I got to third grade or so. Sometimes someone's daddy would come on a field trip or to some lunchtime performance. It became really clear to me then. Like, *oh, so it's just him.* Or maybe it's me."

She chopped and set something that smelled really good on the stove and began to cook. "The trailer we grew up in had two bedrooms. Eight kids and two bedrooms. You can imagine what that was like I'm sure. Or maybe not. I hope not, actually. Anyway, it was pretty much impossible to hide from him when he got angry. Unless you just left. Which I did as much as I could. Lily's parents had me stay over a lot. That's where I learned that normal kids didn't sleep under their beds to hide from dad when he got so drunk he needed to hurt someone just to ease himself."

He'd known they'd had a hardscrabble life. Knew about the drinking and the catting around. But he'd had no idea the depth of it. William had never said. He'd never asked either. "Jesus."

"No. Not in my trailer. My mother was no help. She's an alcoholic too. A bigger mess than my dad in some ways. Her biggest addiction is attention. From lots of men who aren't my dad. She'd run off for days, sometimes weeks. Sometimes he'd go to find her. Sometimes he'd stay home and drink. His temper was always worse when he drank. He's mean, my father. But when he's drinking he's cruel. Tate was his favorite target because, as you can tell, she's not his. The rest of us are tall with dark hair. Like him. But Tate is short and blonde. She was always so full of love for us, protected us. He resented that and my mother did too in her own way. She never protected us. She lied to the cops. Lied to the doctors when we got broken bones or had to go to the emergency room.

"We got good at lying too. It was easier, you see, if we just went along with the fiction. We fell down the steps, or ran into a door. Tate would dumpster dive for clothes because we never had any. We didn't have coats for the cold. She managed to make a connection at the thrift store. She cleaned up after they closed and they let her have stuff for us. William and Tim had jobs, so we could eat."

She stirred, adding garlic and vegetables to the meat, and his stomach growled, despite his growing horror.

"My parents wouldn't allow us to go on the school lunch

program. They didn't want anyone to think they couldn't take care of their kids." Her laugh was bitter.

"Tate stepped in between me and a fist more times than I can count. She, William and Tim paid hush money to my parents to let us live in the apartment they'd rented. And each one of us, once we could get a job, we helped with the younger ones. That's what you do when you love your family."

"I'm sorry. I'm sorry I didn't know. I..."

She held up a hand. "I know how to make spaghetti, that's what's for dinner, by the way. I know how to make it because Tate taught me. It was easy and relatively cheap. Kept you going all day. We ate it a lot in that little apartment Tate, Tim and William rented. For about six years after I got out of school and had a job, I refused to eat spaghetti. Every time I heard the burble of boiling pasta, or smelled spaghetti sauce, all I could think of were those fists. Of sweat filled with the stench of hopelessness and alcohol. I refused to speak of what my life was like. For a long time I refused to deal with it. I hid it, was ashamed of what I'd come from because it made me feel weak."

"You can't possibly think it's your fault." He was so angry he wanted to drive over to that trailer and beat the shit out of her father.

"I don't. Not now." She buttered bread and put it on a cookie sheet. "For a long, long time I did. I think it wasn't until Tate got together with Matt that I was truly able to let it go. She got the happily-ever-after that she deserved. It made me reevaluate.

"When I was four, my father broke my arm. It was one of the few times we ever had a Christmas tree. Guilt. So he and my mother got into it. A week before Christmas. She set the tree on fire."

"Your father broke your arm?"

"Yes. And he knocked out one of my front teeth. He beat me so bad I had to ditch school. More than once. We were raised, you see, to believe that if people knew what happened in that trailer they'd send us to juvie. Juvie was jail. We'd be separated and put in jail. I believed that for a long, long time. So we kept silent. And we hid what we came from. In varying degrees, we held ourselves responsible for the sins of other people who should have known better."

She held his gaze. "I am not responsible for the thug my father is. I am not responsible that he's quick with his fists and slow with his labor. I am not responsible for my mother. Or for the fact that Tate is not his. Or for the fact that I have running water and electricity and half the time they don't. You can't be responsible for other people's shit, Joe. If there's one thing in the world I know to be totally true, it's that. You are not responsible for your father's mental illness. Hiding it, or being ashamed of it won't make it go away. Punishing yourself by breaking up with your girlfriend—who loves you—well, that's not going to make it go away either."

"Beth, you can't love me."

"Shut the fuck up." She slid the pasta into the water, stirring as she held her tongue.

He reeled in more than one way. Her story, Jesus. And her declaration of love.

She turned to face him. "I understand shame. I understand fear and helplessness over people's behavior and their health problems."

She dug through her bag and tossed a thick stack of papers on the table. "Trey's sister is a mental-health nurse. Buck and I had breakfast with her. There are some resources here. Names and places your dad can maybe find the help he needs. I don't know all the details of course. She didn't give me

166

any diagnoses or anything like that. But she did say that it often happened that it might take a few tries to find the right course of treatment. This is brain-chemistry stuff, it takes tinkering to find the right medications and the right amounts. It's easy, she told me, to get discouraged. But that the overwhelming percentage of the time they can find something that works."

Joe looked through the papers. He had most of the information already from his research. There were some new things, though. And more than that, she'd done it for him. She'd gone out and spent the time and effort. To help his dad who'd tried to hurt her. To help Joe, who'd broken her damned heart and acted like a dick.

It touched him that she cared so much. That she'd not only told him she loved him, but showed she truly did.

Guilt rushed through him.

"I appreciate all this. I do. But it doesn't change things between us." He stood and gathered her things. "You need to go. I meant it when I broke things off. I have too much to deal with right now. My dad is the reason I came back here to Petal. I need to work to pay the bills, yes, but all my time needs to be spent on him. It's not fair to him, or to you, to try to have a girlfriend on top of that. Maybe later...after this is settled. I don't know."

He opened his door. "Thank you for dinner. I should invite you to stay to eat it, but I don't want to confuse things any more than they're already confused."

"*Confused?* Bullshit. This isn't confusion. I'm not confused. Neither are you, for that matter. Don't do this, Joe. I can help you with all of this. Support you. I don't need you to be with me twenty-four hours a day. But damn it, you need someone to take care of you when you get run-down. You need to be able to turn to someone when things get rough. That's what I'm here for."

"I have to, Beth. And if you care about me like you say you do, you'll get the fuck out of here and leave me be. I need to put my energy and focus on my dad. I can't be with you. Don't make it harder than it is already."

"It's not either/or. I can help you. I want to help you. You can lean on me, trust me. I love you, dumbass."

"I am a dumbass." He snorted. "But I can't divide my attention. It's not right. I was a shitty son. A horrible, selfish jerk and I need to not be that guy."

She bent to scratch Buck's ears. "See you around, Buck." She took the bags at the door. "You know where I am when you realize you're being stupid."

He shook his head. "We don't have a future. You need to move on. Don't wait around for me." He gently pushed her out and closed the door, watching through the peephole as she went to her car and drove away.

Buck growled at him, turned and walked off.

"I know. Okay? I know. But you heard her story. She doesn't need any more fucked-up stuff in her life. She deserves a guy with a normal life. I can't be that. Even if and when my dad gets himself straight, it'll always be there. I can't saddle her with any more crap. I'm doing it for her. And for me and my parents too. I have to do the right thing, Buck."

"So how goes it?" It was her lunch hour and she'd escaped to the Honey Bear. Apparently William was still around, as he was the one who'd brought her lunch out to her.

He slid into a seat across from hers.

"What do you mean?"

He rolled his eyes. "Baby girl, I'm your big brother. You're nursing a broken heart. How are things on the Joe front?"

It had been two weeks since that day when Joe had kicked her out of his apartment after she'd told him the story of her childhood. She hadn't told anyone that part. It had felt like a rejection of her and of that story for a while. She wasn't so sure now, but it still hurt.

"He wanted some space, I'm trying to give it to him. You know more than I do. He doesn't talk to me."

"He loves you." William stole one of her potato chips. "I shouldn't tell you any of this because, to be honest, I'm not sure if Joe is right for you. I got a problem with a man who can't see what's right in front of his face. But you love him and I love you and I want you to be happy. He's drowning in all the stuff with his father. Court stuff for that night at the Sands. More mental-health evaluations. His dad is resisting. His mom has checked out of the process."

She sipped her tea. "I hate that he's doing this on his own. I've gone by the shop but he won't talk to me. I stopped by his place but he won't open the door. I sent food over a few times. I know he took it. Jacob told me. I can't do it on my own."

"He doesn't want you to have to get tied up in any of this stuff."

"I told him." She blurted it.

"What?"

"I told him about our childhood. About the drinking and the beating. I wanted him to understand that I got it. You know? I wanted him to see that I understood what it was to be ashamed of what people did, even when it wasn't your fault. And he shoved me out of his house and hasn't spoken to me since."

William moved to sit next to her, putting an arm around her shoulder. "Sweetheart, what Joe is doing is stupid, yes. But it's not about you. Not about you telling him about what happened in that trailer. Is that what you think?"

"I don't know what to think. I want to fix things. But he won't let me. He keeps pushing me away. I love him. I want to help him but he won't let me. He won't even just be with me at all. It's hard not to feel like he's rejected me because of that story."

"Have you never told it before?"

"What we went through? Some, here and there. It's been years since I've stayed silent. We all told Matt and the Chases some. And here and there it comes up. I've never hidden it from someone I dated, but I've never gone into the detail I did with Joe. None of them have been important enough for me to expose that part of my life that way. I wanted him to understand what it meant that I was sharing. I wanted it to make a difference and it didn't."

"How do you know it didn't? Hm? How do you know he didn't hear that story and think, that girl's got enough damage, I can't give her any more."

"Why would he think that? That's dumb."

William laughed. "We're men, my wife tells me this all the time. We do dumb stuff thinking we're doing the right thing, but we just mess things up. He's a guy. He's buried in all this mental-health stuff. He wants to keep you away from it."

"He thinks he was a bad son."

"He *was* a bad son." William snorted a laugh. "He wants to make amends and he's doing that. He's doing what he should with his family. Being a real man. He's got to do this." He kissed the top of her head. "But that doesn't mean you can't send him a little jolt."

"Yeah? What do you mean?"

"Keep showing up. Keep yourself in his sights. He needs to know you're not going anywhere. You're too stubborn."

"You think that'll make any difference?"

"Way I see it, you can give up and move on. Or you can keep trying. You can't mope around. It makes me want to punch him. He's my best friend so I'd rather not. But you're my baby sister and he's the one making you this way. I can't have that."

She smiled up at her brother. Usually so gruff. "I can't remember the last time I've heard you say this much at one time."

"I hate to see you sad. You deserve a man who makes you smile. If it's not going to be him, move on. I'll help you however I can. But you're my kooky, smiling sister. I want my Beth back."

"You're very sweet."

"Don't tell anyone."

"Your secret really isn't that much of a secret. Especially if they've seen you with your children for more than a minute."

He rolled his eyes, but she saw his smile, knew he was warmed by her compliment. "We can move past what we came from. We can let it make us better instead of hobbling us and dragging us down."

"I love you." She hugged him.

"I love you too."

She stopped by the garage after she left the Honey Bear. Jacob saw her, as did Buck, who barked, dancing over.

"You're like one of those dancing horses, Buck. I've missed

171

you." She had a cookie in her pocket so she passed him one, which he inhaled and then gave her a few kisses in thanks. "Where's your dad?"

"Beth, why are you here?"

She stood, and the way his gaze ate her up gave her hope she hadn't had much of before then. He missed her. *Ha.*

"I'm here to say hello to my brother. And to see Buck. I have a stash of dog cookies at work and it would be a crime to let them go to waste."

Jacob left, leaving her alone with Joe. He had dark spots under his eyes.

"You're not sleeping enough."

"Beth."

"What? Come on, Joe, this is so silly. I know you care about me. You know I care about you. How's your father?"

"He's fine. Or, on his way to being fine. Hopefully. You need to go."

"You're still playing this? You want to touch me. I can tell."

"I want a lot of things I can't have. I can't afford you, Beth."

"I'm already yours. You know that."

He swallowed hard, not speaking for long moments. "You need to move on. I'm going to as well. I never should have let things get serious between us. It was a mistake. You and I were a mistake."

She knew he was using it to hold her back, but it hurt anyway.

"You're a liar. And a coward. Two things I'd never have thought of you before now."

"Another two reasons for you to move on then. Go, Beth. I have too much. Too many things and people depending on me. I can't have a girlfriend. You're more than a casual fuck. That's not a lie. But I can't have anything more than that. I'm moving on and you should too."

Honestly? If she saw him out with another woman she might have to run him down with her car. She considered telling him that, but then she thought he'd do it to try to push her away harder.

"I'll be seeing you around. Get some sleep, why don't you?" She bent, giving him a view right down the front of her sweater. He may as well get a little memory of what he could have if he wasn't a dick. "Buck, make him get some sleep."

She turned, swaying out, looking back over her shoulder and finding him staring longingly at her ass. "See you around, Joe Harris."

Chapter Fourteen

Lily shook her head. "He's not worth it."

"I disagree." Tate sighed, rubbing her stomach. "He's hurting. She knows it. She wants to make it better. I think her plan has merit."

"I think her plan is dumb. Why should she have to do any of this at all? If he loves her so much, why should she have to do more than she is already doing? She sends him food. She asks after him and he won't even talk to her! Fuck him." Anne shrugged. "I agree with Lily. Beth is better than this jerk. She should move on. There are other guys in town."

"And none of them is Joe." Tate cocked her head. "Right?"

Beth blew out a breath. "Not a one."

"He loves her. William says so. I say so. Anyone with eyes says so." Tate waved in Beth's direction. "We gonna let this guy push our Beth away?"

"Maybe we should! He doesn't deserve her," Anne growled. "He makes her sad and I don't like it. Not one bit."

"If this doesn't work, I vote we *all* make him sad. Forever and ever. But, our Beth wants him. And I think he does deserve her. He's hurting. We all know what that feels like." Tate looked to Lily, who sighed. "If you hadn't given Nathan a second chance, how would your life be? Hm?"

"You fight dirty." Lily frowned and then turned to Beth. "You're too good for him."

"Of course she is. That goes without saying. She'd be too good for any man."

Beth squeezed Tate's hand.

"What if he doesn't respond?"

"He needs a jolt. That's what William said. I showed up at the garage and started that ball rolling. He couldn't take his eyes off my boobs or my butt. That's step one. Plus, he saw me, spoke to me, he got a good old reminder of why he loves me. So now he needs to remember there are people who love him. Who want to help him. That he can have a life outside all this stuff with his dad and still be a good son. And, he needs to realize that I won't wait around forever. If he doesn't wake the hell up, I can find a man elsewhere."

She took a deep breath.

"And if he doesn't respond? I'll know it's really time for me to move on."

Trey looked up when she cruised through the door of his and Jacob's apartment. "Just the man I wanted to see."

He gave her a look. A little scared at the edges and she nearly felt sorry for him. "What? Jacob isn't here."

"I know." She plopped down on the couch next to him, putting her feet up. "You should take me on a date."

He coughed. "Darlin', what about me makes you think I've got a death wish?"

"I'm very pretty. And I'm funny. And, I have it under good authority that my boobs are nice."

He clapped a hand over his eyes. "No. Way. Your brother

175

would kill me, no matter how nice your, um, whatever, may be. Plus, Joe. No way. Nuh-uh. No how."

She sighed. "I need your help. Please."

He took his hand away and looked at her, groaning. "You know I can't take that tone."

She did. And again, she nearly felt bad for using it. But not bad enough.

"Do you want to help me or not?"

"If Joe punches me in the face, you have to pay my medical bills."

"If he tries to punch you in the face, I'll know he still wants me."

He sighed. "Girl, he wants you. Good God, how can you even doubt that? Lemme tell you, since it's become public info that you two broke up, the place is swimming with women making googly eyes at him. He doesn't notice a single one of them. No matter how low-cut the tops are. Plus, Buck tries to bite them."

She laughed, delighted. "Really?"

"Really."

"I still need you to take me out and pretend you like me."

"This stuff is high stakes, Beth."

"Don't you think I know that? I've tried. It's been a month. *An entire month* since we broke up. I've given him space. I've tried to poke around gently. I've tried being pushy. I've tried pretending that it doesn't matter. But it does. I'm desperate."

He scrubbed hands over his face. "I'm going to be so sorry for this."

She fluttered her lashes. "Nuh-uh. You'll have the knowledge that you helped true love find a way."

"Yeah, five fingers of it in a fist, planted in my face. Your boyfriend is huge."

She laughed. "It'll be fine. I promise. Now, here's what we need to do."

Two nights later, they sat in a booth up against the front windows of the Sands. Beth figured Joe probably wouldn't come back there after the whole thing with his dad, though she knew Roni had refused to press charges. Joe had paid for the replacement glass and Roni cared about his dad, not jail time.

But it was on the way between the garage and most everything else in town. If he walked past, he'd see her. She wore a bright red sweater with a vee neck. She and Lily had gone and picked up an awesome push-up bra that had her girls mounded nicely at the neckline. Hell, even Trey had looked a few times and he professed to be scared for his life.

Tate had done her hair so it was tousled in waves, long and lush all around her face. Anne had done her makeup and had even given her fake eyelashes. She'd looked at herself in the mirror, in her jeans and that sweater, with her eyes lined all smoky and sexy with the lashes and red lips. "If he doesn't respond to this, I may have to finally admit it's over."

"Are you kidding me? Gurl, I'm straight and marrying your brother and I'd look twice. Hell, your boobs are so hot I can't stop looking." Lily had waggled her brows. Of course Trey had nearly tripped, and then he'd cursed under his breath and tried to keep his gaze anywhere else.

She didn't eat much. Enough people had seen them that even if Joe didn't walk by, and he hadn't so far, he'd hear about it the next day. She had no guilt about using the power of a small town to her advantage. Gossip moved lightning fast. And she knew those hoochies sniffing around her man would find a way to tell him if no one else did.

"I haven't seen him," Trey said. "I'm sorry. You sure do look pretty tonight."

"I'm so bummed I'm not even hungry for pie." She did smile at him though. May as well put on a show.

"That smile of yours makes me feel like a rabbit and you're the wolf."

She laughed then, relaxing. He'd make some woman a good match. He was cute and smart and he made her laugh. He was also too young and a lot like family.

"Wouldn't do to go out with a new man and mope around. No. If he's going to go home and hide without walking past, he'll still hear we were here. And I want him to hear how much I smiled and laughed."

"You're diabolical."

She *tsk*ed. "Of course I am. My goodness, Trey, is this a surprise?"

"I guess not. You always seem so nice and funny."

"I *am* nice and funny. Which is why Joe Harris loves me. But if a girl isn't willing to use all she's got to fight for her man, what use is she as a partner in life? Hm? Nice is great. But I'm resourceful."

He laughed, taking her hand and kissing it. "How's that?"

"Nicely done. How about a beer? I can use one. My treat for spending your night with me."

He got out first, holding an arm for her to grab. "Don't tell Jacob, but it's been fun. Anyway, it can't hurt for the ladies of Petal to see me with a pretty woman on my arm. Raises my value."

"Like a house with a pool."

They laughed, walking arm in arm over to the Pumphouse. It was a Friday night so the place was full. The pool tables in the back were likely to already have a wait. The jukebox was humming, and it made Beth remember that there was a life outside her mopey little world.

Some folks got up and she saw the opening at the table. "Oh, look. A table just opened."

"Grab it. I'll be back in a second with beer. My treat, not yours. Jeez."

She grinned, settling in as she looked around. Well, what do you know? She'd recognize that gorgeous head of hair and long, tall body anywhere. Joe was in the back with William and the Chase boys playing pool.

The night was looking up. She shimmied from her coat, adding some extra shimmy, just in case he looked over.

When Trey came back with a pitcher and two glasses, she smiled.

"Joe is here. In the back." He said this in an undertone, getting close.

"I know. I just saw him. Okay, Trey, act like I make you tingly."

He choked and she had to pat him on the back.

"The stuff you say. My God. You probably aged Joe five years."

"But they were really good five years, Trey." She winked.

Joe bent to take his shot, glad he'd decided to accept the invitation to play pool and drink beer. It had been way too long.

Something caught his attention near the front. It was the lush red of the sweater first. Then the tits. Holy crap. Immediately he felt guilty. He might be broken up with Beth, but he shouldn't be oogling anyone else's boobs. And then he tore his gaze away, past those tits and up. It was the hair. Thick dark caramel.

It was Beth, her head bent toward none other than Trey! Trey, who was also caught up in those magnificent boobs.

He held her hand. A hand Joe used to hold. And kissed her fingertips while she laughed prettily. God, probably saying something dirty and sexy.

"You gonna take that shot or just bend over the table for a while?" William asked this lazily, as he sipped his beer.

"Did you know about that?" He jerked his head in Beth's direction before taking a shot he missed terribly.

He noted the surprise on his friend's face. He hadn't known.

"I didn't. But I don't know why you're surprised. She's been trying to get you back for over a month and you keep telling her to move on. I guess she finally decided to."

"Sweet baby Jesus. No offense, William, but your sister is looking mighty fine tonight. And you?" Royal looked to Joe. "You're a dumbass for letting that slip through your fingers."

"Says the guy who chases after Anne."

"Says the guy who has finally decided to take her no as a no and move on. Maybe I've been looking at the wrong sister all along."

The thought of Beth in Royal Watson's bed on a Saturday morning, naked and warm? No.

Joe scoffed. It was either that or punch his friend for even imagining such a thing. "Dream on. Beth would never get anywhere near you in a romantic sense. They have that sister code."

Royal's expression told Joe he knew exactly the response

his claim would evoke. "She's in love with you anyway. *For now.* That's not going to last forever. I have no idea why you're over here when she's just over there looking like a shiny Christmas ornament."

"I don't have time for a relationship."

"You already had a relationship with her." William took his shot. "You're messing up, Joe. Royal is right. She's not going to wait around forever."

He watched, sullen, as she talked and laughed with Trey until he leaned over, whispered in her ear, and she nodded, her eyes going half-mast.

She got up and he helped her into her coat. Near the door she looked back over her shoulder, straight at Joe.

She *knew* him, damn it. That shock of recognition zinged through him. But he didn't move. She shrugged and let Trey pull her out the doors and onto the sidewalk where he slung an arm around her shoulder and they walked away.

He'd still been thinking when William shoved him.

Hands pulled at the two of them, shouting to calm down.

"What the fuck?"

"You just gonna stand there while the best thing that ever happened to you walks away? What is wrong with you, Joe? You said you came back here to start fresh. You're acting like such a dumbass."

"I..."

"I told her, damn you. I told her that you were worth fighting for. But that if you didn't wise up I was going to have to punch your face for making her sad. I also said I'd hate to do it since you were my best friend and all. But you're making me regret that last bit." William's eyes had narrowed.

Nathan sighed as he put a hand on his brother's shoulder a

moment before speaking to Joe. "Originally, I tried to warn Beth off. I told her you weren't the kind of dude she needed to be with. She told me what she thought of you. And through her, I realized that maybe you *were* what she needed. You came here and helped out your family. Oh get that look off your face. We know what's going on. I know she told you about our childhood and I know you pushed her out the door after that. She risked something and you rejected her."

It hit him then and he swallowed back nausea. He shook his head, hard. "I didn't reject her for that. That's not true. I'd *never* do that. Does she think that? If she did, why did she keep coming around to check on me?"

"She loves you for starters. And she doesn't think you rejected her because of that. Though I think she might have thought it for a while. You tell me, Joe Harris. You think long and hard and you tell me what other woman on this planet who'd be better for you than Beth. What woman would support you and help you? She's there for you. You and I both know it and you let her walk out those doors. I don't know what your problem is. But I will tell you this is go time. Either go get her, or let her go for good."

Joe put his cue back and grabbed his coat, heading for the doors. Not to go get her, but to take a ride. Yes, he needed to get the hell away from town and all the Murphys for a while.

He drove back home to grab his gear. When he opened the closet, he saw her helmet on the shelf next to his. He grabbed his and Buck barked.

"What?"

The dog sat, his tongue lolling as he took Joe in.

"I'm going for a ride to clear my head. It's dry enough."

Buck just kept looking at him.

"It's a good thing she's moving on. I mean, I'm not what she needs."

Buck snorted, got up, gave Joe his butt and walked away.

"Whatever."

He was arguing with a dog. This is what his life had sunk to? He got the bike out, driving slowly out of town before opening her up and roaring through the night.

She needed someone else. Hadn't he told her that?

Of course she'd argued that *he* was the one for her. And he'd refused her. She'd sure moved on easily enough.

Okay, that wasn't fair. He knew she'd tried to get him back. But if she was dating now it meant she'd accepted that they couldn't be together. It was what he wanted.

Maybe.

Maybe it was more about what she needed. Right? Shouldn't he be the bigger person here and do what was best for her? He had baggage.

She was a beautiful woman. Successful. Family centered. It wasn't hard to see why a guy like Trey would be interested in her. It was good she was getting past Joe. There were men in Petal who could give her what she needed.

She needed...

He thought back to Beth telling him she needed *him*. Who was he to tell her what she needed when she seemed to know so strongly?

The truth was, he needed her. He could admit it as he rode alone in the dark. Needed her so much just the thought of her got him through many a rough spot in the last month.

She made him laugh. She didn't take him seriously when he was pissy. Took a strong person with a sense of herself to blow off someone's mood the way she did. It disarmed him.

He thought about her sense of humor. Bawdy. He loved that part of her. When it was just the two of them, she could be so dirty. Carnal. He was sure he'd never laughed so much and had so much great sex too.

More than that and just in general, she had a quick wit. An easy way with her siblings and friends. She was the one who tended to run interference when tempers flared. She diverted anger and annoyance and teased it away. William or Nathan got gruff and she handled them. They knew it, of course, but she was impossible to resist. If Beth wanted you to smile, it was pretty hard not to.

He growled inside his helmet.

Beth Murphy was a strong woman. A helpmate, his mother would have called it. She was the kind of woman a man could come together with at the end of the day and share with.

The kind of woman who'd kick a man's ass six ways to Sunday if he acted a fool, but who'd defend him to the death when he was right. She was ferocious when it came to the people she cared about.

Strong. He'd never looked at her as another responsibility. Though he cared about her, she didn't need him the way his mother did. She was her own person. Independent.

The way she'd gone out and done all that research, how she'd contacted Trey's sister to get him more information about mental-health treatment and resources—it had touched him then, and over the month they'd been apart, he'd thought about it more and more.

She'd seen a need and had jumped to fill it. Though he'd dumped her. She'd done it, had brought him food. Had made him dinner while she had opened up some really private parts of her life to make a point.

And it had been a damned good point. At the time, he'd been so wrapped up in his dad and his guilt and shame that he hadn't really seen all the facets to that story she'd told him about her life.

More than just a way to prove her point about not carrying other people's actions, it showed him how tender she was. Despite the horror she'd grown up with. Despite enduring stuff that would make most people hard and angry, she was not.

She'd done nothing but show him love. Kindness and compassion. At the same time, she'd shown spine to keep coming back. Even as he rejected her over and over. She'd encouraged him to keep fighting to find the right course of treatment for his father. Even as he'd stopped answering his door when she came over.

She gave and gave without expecting anything in return. She did it because he needed it.

That was love.

He pulled off to the side of the road and yanked his helmet off.

"Fuck. Fuck. Fuck."

If he let Beth go he was a total moron.

He loved Beth Murphy. Loved her persistence. Her strength. Her humor. Her sexy walk. The way she just bulldogged her way through everything. He'd never in his life met a more stubborn woman.

And it worked.

He put his helmet back on, turned the bike around and headed back to Petal.

Chapter Fifteen

"Man oh man, he's totally going to hurt me tomorrow." Trey cast quick glances at the back where Joe was.

"He won't. He's got too much pride. Anyway, when he finally wises up, I'll let him know it was just a way to poke at him and then he won't want to hurt you anymore."

He'd better wise up. Here she was looking absolutely freaking gorgeous, sitting with another man who totally couldn't stop looking at her boobs. If Joe didn't come over to their table and declare how stupid he was being, she...well, she might just give up.

They chatted as they drank their beer. People stopped by their table to chitchat. Mostly though because the whole damned town knew she and Joe had broken up and that he was in the back playing pool. The drama of it was too delicious to pass up.

Whatever. She had no intention of giving them a show. That would have been too much like her parents.

"People in this town are nosy."

She smiled at Trey. "No one can resist the excitement. This is going to be all over town tomorrow. Maybe I made a mistake doing this."

Trey took her hand, kissing her fingertips. It brought her

words to a halt. He gave her such a wicked grin too, knowing that he'd gotten her a tiny bit tangled up.

He laughed. "Ha! See, I can do it too. Now you listen here, if that dumbass back there doesn't come to his senses, you're better off without him. I'm not playing now. You intended to give him a lesson about how beautiful and desirable you were. That if you took his advice to move on, this is what it would look like. It's got to be hard to swallow, a man like him. But he needed to understand what his words would mean. As for all over town? Well yeah. It's Petal after all. But look, it would have been anyway, no matter who you started dating. There are only so many places in town to take a date. It would be bound to happen."

"Thanks, coach. That was a good speech."

"You use humor to push stuff away too, I know your game."

"You're right, of course. Really, thank you. I hope I don't have to start dating anyone else. It would suck to break in someone else. All that work with Joe down the drain. Plus, I like the man's dog. And his motorcycle. He orders extra cake when we go out so I can have it."

"If that's not love, I don't know what is."

"So is he looking over here? I'm trying to act like I'm caught up in your sexitude so I can't look."

"My sexitude? Cripes. Yes, he's looking. Frowning. Glowering. William has looked too. They're talking about you. That much is clear."

They stayed a while longer but that butthead didn't come over.

"Let's go. It's loud in here and I'm tired and if he's going to make his move, he might need the push of me leaving."

Trey leaned in a lot closer. "Maybe if he thinks we're going back to your place to smooch, you'll push him that last bit."

Beth put on a little show for Joe, letting her eyes slide halfway closed. "Or more. We, Joe and me I mean, have some smoking hot chemistry in bed. If he thought I was giving that to you..." She shrugged, sliding from her chair and letting Trey help her into her coat.

She flipped her hair back over her shoulder, knowing how much Joe loved her hair, and turned, locking her gaze with his, feeling that connection they had straight to her toes.

Beth willed him to come over. Willed him to just admit he needed her.

But he stood there, not making a move.

She covered her disappointment the best she could, turning and letting Trey lead her outside.

"I surely did think that last thing you did would get him. Hard to resist a woman when she does that thing with her hair."

Trey was a sweetie pie. She smiled at him and tried not to cry.

He slung an arm around her shoulders. "Don't cry, doll. Don't let him see your tears. I'll take you home."

She heard the motorcycle and her heart skipped. She'd tried to sleep and had ended up watching *Mary Poppins* instead. Eating an entire bag of Doritos and drinking two Cokes. Diet, naturally, as if that would combat the eleven billion Doritos calories.

So she was zinged up from caffeine and boyfriend annoyance, and it had taken five minutes to scrub the orange from her fingertips.

Sitting on her couch in her pajamas, she listened to the sound of the engine cutting and wondered what to do. It'd been nearly four hours since she'd left the Pumphouse. *Four hours.* He'd taken his sweet time. She could be sleeping! She could be sleeping with another man in her bed for all he knew.

She frowned.

She should just not answer her door. Yes. It would serve him right if she told him to fuck off and turned the porch light off.

She rolled her eyes at herself. She'd open the door, even if just to see his face, to know he was all right. But that didn't mean she was going to make it easy.

Still, she made herself wait until she heard the knock before she got up, keeping her pace to the door under a rush.

She opened it and he stood there, looking so beautiful she had to fist her hands to keep from touching him. She remained in the doorway, blocking his path.

"Hi. Did I wake you?" He looked her over.

"It's one in the morning."

"I know." He shoved a hand through his hair, sending it into disarray, and she wanted to fix it. But she couldn't fix this. He had to want to fix it himself.

"What are you doing here?"

"Are you alone? I mean, is there anyone else…"

She looked him up and down. Did he really, truly think that even a month away from him would be enough to fuck someone else?

"No. I guess there isn't. You're not that type. I mean, I hope…" He licked his lips as she kept him standing there. "I'm not doing this right."

"Five minutes ago you weren't doing it at all."

One of her brows rose and he wanted so very much to kiss it. Wanted to draw her into his arms and hold her tight, tell her with words and with his body that he would never fuck up again. That he loved her.

"I went for a ride. I was about ninety minutes out when I realized. No, when I accepted the truth. I had to come back and then I needed to get gas and then I drove around wondering if I should wait until the morning and then I wondered if you were alone and I knew you were, of course, but it was killing me, imagining Trey with his lips on yours, his hands on your body when it was my fault it wasn't my hands instead."

He halted, looking at her. She blocked his way, but she hadn't slammed the door in his face. So there was that.

"You're mad."

"Yes."

"*You* came into the Pumphouse on a date. A date, Beth. And *you're* mad?"

"I'm going to help you. This one time. This is not a useful or helpful line of argument for you."

She was so icy and fierce, it made him hot. Christ, he was in so deep with her.

"You're right. I'm sorry."

"For what?"

"Can I come in? It's cold out here."

"I'm sure you were colder on the bike. Also? No. Maybe later if I like what you have to say. But you're nowhere near being invited in at this point."

Damn.

"Can I tell you it makes me hot to see you this way?"

"No."

He sighed, licking his lips again.

"I'm sorry for being an ass and not seeing what is so plainly right in front of my face. You. Beth. I love you. It doesn't matter what I tell myself about how much baggage I have. It doesn't matter that I tell myself that you're better off with someone else. Because I love you. I love you so much and I messed up so badly and I hurt you."

"You didn't believe in me. Or us."

"I was so caught up in everything else that I couldn't risk it. Didn't want to risk it."

She leaned against the doorjamb, watching. She looked a little less like she planned to knee him in the junk, which was a step forward at least.

"I was ashamed. Scared as hell."

"Ashamed of your dad?"

He nodded. "It's better now. I've had a few sessions with a therapist too. My mom as well. I understand it better. I guess you knew it all along. But it took me a while to get there."

She blinked quickly, he knew tears were close and hated that he'd done it.

"You shared yourself with me. Took a risk and opened up such a private part of yourself and I didn't...I wasn't appreciative of it. Not to you and I should have been. I should have let you know how much it meant that you came to me that day. I did appreciate it. It did help. A lot. But I should have told you then. I made you feel bad. That I pushed you away because of that story. And it wasn't true. I'd never do that."

"At first I felt like that, yes. I told you something I rarely talk about. Not that I hide it, but I don't go around laying out my fucked-up childhood for all and sundry."

"I know. I was messed up that day. I...it felt like if I didn't

191

push you out the door that I'd never be able to keep up my strength in protecting you from the insanity of my life. And I shouldn't have. I should have gone with my gut instinct, which was to pull you close and never let go."

She sucked in a breath and stepped back. "You can come in." She turned and walked back inside, leaving him on her doorstep.

Grateful.

He walked inside and noted she'd been on her couch watching movies.

"Thanks. For letting me come in, I mean."

He hung his jacket up and came into the room.

She moved to sit back on the couch, pulling the blanket around herself. To keep him back because she wasn't ready yet. All the things he'd said had mattered. A lot. But there was more that needed saying.

"In all my life, I've never let anyone who wasn't my sibling get as close as I let you get." She played with the hem on the blanket, noting that she needed to fix where it was beginning to fray.

Instead of the chair, he sat next to her. Giving her a little space, but not as much as she liked. She could smell him this close. Could look and see the jump of his pulse at his throat. She knew what that felt like against her mouth. Knew the taste of his skin, the warmth he gave off.

She'd missed him much more than she'd been willing to let herself admit. It rolled over her with such force she had to close her eyes for long moments to keep herself together.

"I've been working so hard to get you to see. To see me. To understand how much I loved you that I guess it didn't hit me until now. Your absence, I mean."

He scooted a little closer, but she put her hands under the blanket.

"I'm sorry. I hate seeing you this way. I want to fix it. I want to touch you. God, I've missed you."

"Not yet." She looked up at him, feeling a little more together. "You don't get to touch me. And if you missed me, where have you been?"

"Three days a week I go in to the shop early to get ahead so I can leave at two. I take my dad in to see his therapist. I don't know what goes on, only that it does. And they're watching him more closely now than they did before. One of those days I go to see a therapist of my own. I guess...I guess I had stuff to unload."

"Is it helping?"

"This mix of medication and talk therapy, listen to me, I have all that lingo now, anyway, it seems to be working for him. He hasn't had an episode in three weeks. My mom, she's in therapy with him. One day a week on her own, one with him. She's more steady."

Beth nodded. "I'm relieved. I can't imagine how scary it must have been. Must be." She corrected herself. "But I meant you. Is the therapy helping you?"

He chewed his bottom lip. "I had this anger. A lot of it. Some from the situation with my dad. But a lot from Iraq. I hadn't really realized it until I started getting it all out. It's better. I guess that's really when I started to realize how much difference you made in my life. Once the other shit cleared up, I saw you. In all the places in my life. I kept telling myself you were better off away from the insanity. After all, you had this shit you had to get over, all that stuff from your childhood. Who was I to shovel more on you?"

She snorted. "God, you're so dumb. How many times can I

tell you that I wanted to help? That I wanted to be there in your life to support you through all this stuff?"

"Hey, look, I'm doing the best I can! I did it for you."

"Bull! You did it, yes, and maybe you think you did it for me. But it wasn't for me. I stood in front of you and begged you. It's been a long time since I begged anyone for anything. It wasn't easy. But I did it because I love you. I saw you were hurting and I wanted to help. There was no difference between that night at the Sands and the night before that."

"You saw it! You saw the horror of it. It could have really harmed you, Beth. Don't even say there was no difference. There was all the difference in the world."

She turned to him, hurting on his behalf.

Quick and clever, he grabbed the hand she'd put on her leg, tangling his fingers with hers. Not letting go. And she let him. Let herself accept that just maybe, they could come out of this on the other side together. Stronger. But she had to deal with all the hard stuff or it would fester.

"The truth is it was there, whether I saw it or not. Your dad has a chemical imbalance. It makes him do things he wouldn't otherwise. If he had cancer, would you be as ashamed? Because he's sick either way. He didn't ask for it. You didn't ask for it. But it's there. And it hurts you. And you hid it. My heart breaks to know you suffered through all those months with that knowledge and fear and that you didn't tell me. Were you afraid I'd judge you?"

"I don't know what I did to deserve you, Beth. But thank God for it." He sighed. "I don't know what I felt. To be totally honest, I just, I don't know, survived. I didn't know what was happening. I had to fight my mom's reluctance to rock the boat. Her fear of whatever we'd find out. I had to fight my dad's fear that he was going crazy no matter what. My fear of the unknown. It felt like those hours I had with you were the one right thing in my life. I didn't want to infect that with all the crap from my parents. I failed them. I wanted to be better. And then you came along. I knew I shouldn't have given in, that I needed to keep you back. But I couldn't resist and once I let you in, I couldn't keep you out. Because it was good and right and you made me really happy."

"Okay. Fair enough. Where do we go from here?"

"I saw you tonight with Trey and...and part of me said, *hey look, she's moving on, that's what I told her to do.* Another part said, *hey that's my woman! I'm going to lose her for real if I can't fix things.*"

He looked down to where he held her hand. "It was the last one that won out." He tipped his chin, catching her gaze and feeling that connection between them click back into place. "I love you, Beth. I was a damned fool to push you away. It was dumb to push you away when you have so much to offer. When I *needed* your support and you offered it so freely. All you've ever done for me, you've put me first. Before your own feelings. I want you to know I see that. I understand it and I'm so grateful for it. And for you. I don't deserve you. At all. But I sure do love you more than I can even put into words. If you forgive me, I'll spend every day for the rest of our lives making it up to you."

She'd waited so long for him to say it. To accept it. To see her for who she was and what he meant to her. "You can touch me now."

He moved to her, pulling her from her nest of blankets and into his lap, encircling her with his arms, holding tight.

She hummed, having missed this so very much she desired nothing more than soaking up how good it felt to be in his arms again.

Beth buried her face in his neck, breathing him in and

letting that ease the panic. "I thought you'd never come to your senses."

"You're not the only stubborn one, darlin'. I'm here now, and I'm not going anywhere. Not ever."

She squirmed a little, trying to get closer, and he groaned. "I've missed you. All parts of me."

She felt the part he meant, poking into her behind.

Tipping her head back, she laughed, throwing her arms around his neck. "What are you waiting for then?"

He grinned, bending to kiss her, and she let all her fear go as she opened to him.

At first the kiss was nearly sweet. Reverent. He took it slow until she was just about to throw him to the floor and mount him.

"I'm trying to take my time here." He spoke against her mouth and she nipped his bottom lip.

"Why? Jeez, Joe, give it to me!"

Laughing, he picked her up, and she grabbed on as he carried her to her bedroom. He put her down gently, and she launched herself at him, knocking him back onto the bed, pulling at his clothes as she straddled his waist.

"Someone wants it bad."

She nodded, pulling her shirt up and off, satisfied for a moment by the way his gaze lasered onto her boobs, widening slightly.

He took them in his hands and she arched into his touch.

"I missed these. Though I did get a good look at a lot of them tonight in that sweater. So did Trey. Hope he got an eyeful, because if he looks at 'em like that again, I'll poke him right in the eye."

She laughed as he bucked her off and she landed on her

back. "Though my girls looked *amazing* in that sweater tonight, I should tell you Trey has no romantic interest in me whatsoever."

He pulled off her pajama bottoms and panties. "That sweater should be part of your regular date-night repertoire. He'd better not, or he and I are going to have to have a Come To Jesus about whose boobs are okay to look at. I'm leaving the socks on because they look hot."

Like she'd complain.

He pulled his shirt and then pants and shorts off.

"Damn you're gorgeous. I have missed all that Joe in my bed. Also I've had to use the step stool a lot more. And my vibrator."

He groaned as he insinuated himself between her thighs. She hissed as the wave of pleasure of his skin against hers rolled over her.

"You can't be telling me about your sex toys. I'll explode."

"I might even let you see one or two. After you remind me why you're so much better than silicone, that is."

"I'll get right on that." His mouth found hers again, his tongue sliding between her lips, filling her with his taste. She clutched his shoulders, holding him to her, wrapping her thighs around his waist.

She rolled her hips, trying to get some friction.

"Darlin', easy now. It'll come."

She reached between them, grabbing his cock and squeezing. "Now, now, now." She smeared her thumb through the slick at the tip. "Then you can take it slow."

His breath caught, and then he groaned, licking down her neck. "Impatient."

"Yes. And it's your fault. If you hadn't neglected me so

much I would be far more patient. You need to put this"—she squeezed him again—"in here." She drew the head of his cock through her for just a moment. Enough to make her a little shaky.

"Christ." He reared up, reaching, fumbling through her top drawer until he found a condom, tearing it open with his teeth. She was so hot for him she didn't even lecture him about how it was bad for him to do that.

She pushed him to his back, scrambling over him. He laughed, pulling her back down. "I want you from behind," he said in her ear.

Oh.

She managed to get up on her elbows and knees as he slid fingers through her from behind. "Wanted to be sure you were ready. Oh, sweet, sweet Beth, you are."

"Always for you."

He slowly pushed in, stretching her, trying to take his time. Need clawed at him. Need to thrust in to his balls. Need to claim, to take back and mark. To let them both know she was his now and forever.

A restraining hand at her hip held her as she tried to push back, to take all of him at once. "If you do that, it'll all be over before it starts. It's been over a month since I've been here. It's so good I may pass out. I want to make it good."

She was temptation made a physical thing. Her curves, the pale gleam of her skin, the bumps of her spine as she arched. Her hair slid over the hand he placed at her shoulder, cool and soft.

"I dreamed of this." He pushed in that last bit and paused, simply reveling in her body. In the way they fit. "There's no one else but you, Beth. Always. I've never fit like this with anyone."

He dragged himself nearly all the way out and pressed in again. Over and over. All the way in and then out, her body hugging at him as if she couldn't bear his leaving.

She held him tight, squeezing her muscles around him until he gasped.

"No fair. You're going to push me right over."

Her laugh was breathless.

A challenge.

"Oh, so it's like that? Well all right then." The hand at her shoulder pulled her back as he let go of her hip, circling around to her clit. The sound she made pulled him closer to climax.

She tried to push back against him. To take him deeper and faster, but the hand he kept at her shoulder controlled her movements. He leaned in, kissing her shoulder. "Uh, uh, uh. I'm in charge here."

She nearly melted into a puddle.

She ached. His words had stoked the fire turned raging inferno. He made her feel so beautiful. So desired. Powerful. In the month they'd been apart, she'd been so damned sad and empty. This had been why. She hadn't realized it until that moment when he touched her like she was precious. When he met her with his own need, as he took hers and gave her what she demanded. He filled her up with so much.

Tears pricked her lashes as she accepted the enormity of what it meant to love someone. Of the way it made her vulnerable as she let herself get lost in him. Tangled up in the JoeandBeth of it all.

She flew apart with a cry. A cry he echoed just moments later as he pushed deep and stayed deep.

"Don't you ever leave again. You hear me, Joseph?"

They fell to her mattress, his arms around her, holding her close.

"I hear you, Beth. I hear you. I love you and I'm sure as hell not letting you go ever again. I need you too much."

Chapter Sixteen

Buck ran, his little legs a blur. He grabbed the ball in his mouth and headed back to where Meg giggled and clapped her hands.

Beth, standing against Joe's chest, snorted, amused. "He's gonna get her nice and tired."

"Good for everyone." Joe kissed the top of Beth's head.

"Oh you mean so your son sleeps better too?"

He laughed. "Our son now."

"Did you hear that, Buck? I'm your new mommy."

Meg thought that was hilarious, and Buck danced over, licking Beth's hands, barking up a storm.

"I vote you bring Buck to all family dinners from now on." Matt spoke from where he'd been sitting on the porch with Tate. "He's kept them running all day long. Lots of tired kids will sleep well."

"Well, but now Nicholas is begging for a dog." Maggie snorted. "We were going to the breeder until Beth suggested we try the animal shelter."

"Oh good! Buck was abandoned. Imagine anyone just tossing away a dog as fabulous as he is."

They talked dogs as Beth wandered over to where her sisters sat with Lily and the Chase wives. Polly came out of the house with a tray of hot chocolate and joined them.

"Lily, you're getting married in less than a month." Beth snickered. "And you'll be a Murphy."

"God help you," Anne said, grinning.

"Nathan told me yesterday he wanted to start trying to get pregnant right away. I admit I've been wondering. Holding off on deciding because I wanted Chris to be back on track. But he told me a few days back that he hoped I had a whole passel of kids so he could spoil them."

Nathan had not only been Lily's fiancé, but in a lot of ways he'd stepped in as a father figure to Lily's brother. It had made Nathan a better man, and certainly helped Chris as his own father was sort of a dick.

"Also, I agreed to start looking for a house. Chris will come with us, of course. I told him he would always have a place with me. This way my mom will have her house when she comes home, but Nathan and I can have a house of our own."

That was a huge step, Beth knew. For everyone involved. She also knew Nathan would feel a lot better in a house that was theirs. He'd be at home in a way he never could be at Lily's mom's place.

"Joe asked me to move in with him."

Everyone got quiet, looking her way. Smiles and grins broke out as a flurry of *oh my gods* and *congratulations* sounded.

"When?" Lily demanded. The only person Beth had told was Tate, who she called at five that morning, knowing she'd already be up with Lil Beth.

"Last night at dinner. He just blurted it out. Said we needed to find a place with a big backyard for Buck. He said he wanted to come home to our place every night and know I was there. He wants to make a home with me."

A home.

That's what had done it. She'd made one for herself of course. But with him? With the man she loved in the same town with her family, with her best friends and all the people she loved best in the world?

She'd said yes and wrapped herself around him like a monkey right there in the restaurant.

"He's the one?" Polly asked, taking Beth's hands.

Beth nodded. "Oh yes. He makes everything better. Even dumb stuff like folding laundry and cleaning the bathtub." The latter mainly because he lured her with sex after. But she'd keep that to herself.

"Does he deserve you? I know how hard you fought for him, so clearly you deserve him. But you're special. Not just beautiful on the outside, but on the inside too. We can't have you giving yourself to a man if he's not worthy of you. Edward told me this just the other day. *Polly, make sure our Beth understands how special she is, and how that Joe Harris best be good enough or he'll have me to answer to.*"

"He did?" Edward Chase, a lot like her brothers, made her realize it was entirely possible to be a wonderful husband and father. The way he still looked at Polly, even after nearly four decades of marriage, blew her away. He not only loved her, he loved her ways. Made room for her in his life in a way that was natural and amazing and filled Beth with envy.

"He did. You're like our own daughter too, you know."

"If I can have with Joe, even a shadow of what you and Edward have, I'll consider myself blessed. Joe is a good man. He loves me. He makes sure we always have red licorice and pie. He listens to me and laughs at my jokes. He's good to all my nieces and nephews. Of course it goes without saying his dog is fabulous. And he knows my family is important. It's important to him too. I never thought love could be like this."

"Well then, good. Congratulations, honey. He's one long tall drink of water. Sure will be nice to have another gorgeous man to look at on Sundays for dinner." Polly winked.

That acceptance of this thing with Joe by her family had been important. His family had been amazing as well. Oh, sure, the relationship with his mother was slow. His mother had a whole lot on her plate. It wasn't what Tate had with Polly, but that was all right too. There was only one Polly in the world, anyway.

But his father was doing well on his most recent course of treatment. His mother was accepting that he could be actually getting better. His sister and her kids and husband were coming out for Christmas.

It was good. And strong. Full of promise and laughter. And that was all she could ask for and more.

Girls' Night Out

A Visit to Petal, Part Two

Lauren Dane

Dedication

I write these bonus chapters out of love for these characters and this town. They're a fun treat for those readers who share that love of Petal, the Murphys and the Chase family. Thank you, readers, for being so wonderful.

Chapter One

"I'm just saying that it's a shame to waste all that pretty on a bunch of ladies when you could stay home and use it all up on me."

Maggie looked over to where her husband lounged on the couch, long legs propped up on the coffee table. Even after all the years he'd been hers, he still made her heart kick up every time she looked at him.

Kyle Chase worked with his body. His skin, even in early December, was kissed by the sun. His broad shoulders were muscled from all the landscaping work he did every day.

His hair was in dire need of a cut but she wasn't complaining because it only made him hotter.

She caught his gaze in her reflection after she secured a curl back with a last pin. "I'll still have some pretty left when I get home later. Plus, you have a bachelor party to go to."

He got up and moved to her, *that* look on his face, and she really considered not going to Lily's bachelorette party.

Hands on her hips, he turned her slowly and pulled her close, the heat of him surrounding her, his scent all around. "I think we have some ice cream left. You surely remember how much I like eating it."

Yeah, off her belly. Or the small of her back. A flush worked through her, leaving her faint.

"I do love seeing you get all blurry-eyed over me." He grinned and kissed her long and slow. "We can drop the kids off at my parents' and then come back here instead of going out. I feel a little tickle in my throat."

"Stop being a bad influence."

"Where's the fun in that?"

He stole another kiss and she gave over to it because, well, why not?

"Everyone thinks you're the good one. If they only knew." She laughed as he kissed up her neck, grabbing two handfuls of her behind to keep her close.

"I *am* the good one. That's why you're still with me after all these years despite my crazy family."

Her family now too. The one she'd been born with hadn't been much, but being loved by one Chase meant you got the whole package. Three big, handsome brothers who all had wives she considered her closest friends. A nosy, bossy and loveable mother-in-law, and a father-in-law she was grateful her husband took after. Crazy, yes. Noisy, yes. But she loved each and every one of them and wouldn't want to live a life without them barging into her house at all hours of the day and night.

The kids made noise in the other room, which was pretty much the only thing that enabled her to keep from ripping his jeans open right then and there.

When he pulled back, he still wore that smug guy face. But he deserved to wear it. "You're a menace to all my ladyparts, Kyle Chase."

He laughed. "Good to know, Red."

She brushed her fingertips through the hair at his temples. "Damn, I love that little bit of gray. So sexy."

"No one would even miss us." He kissed her again and she hummed her pleasure.

"You know they would. Your sister-in-law is hosting a party for our dear friend, Lily, and your brothers are all going to a party for our other dear friend. It's not all night, you know." Her mother-in-law would be keeping the kids overnight so they had plenty of time to get loud and then sleep in afterward.

"Fine. Go on and be responsible and reasonable." He kissed her forehead. "I'll drop the kids off on my way to meet the guys over at the Tonk. If anyone gets fresh, let Tate at them. She's scary. Especially when she's pregnant."

Maggie laughed. "We're going to sit around, eat too much, talk about sex and laugh. It's the back room at the Pumphouse, it'll just be us anyway."

He stepped back with a reluctant sigh. "I'll see you later. There *will* be ice cream and your belly." One of his brows went up as she fought for her breath. "And my tongue. Just sayin'."

"Can't wait." She gulped. "You're a scoundrel. You know that, right?"

His answering grin told her he did. And thank goodness he was *her* scoundrel. Their sons were so like him. Good gracious she was going to end up like Polly in a few decades!

"Whatever are you thinking?" He brushed the pad of his thumb over her temple, and she leaned into his touch.

"Nothing bad. Don't get that panicked face. I was thinking about how the boys were exactly like you and how I'd be like your mother by the time they grew up."

He wrinkled his nose. "Well if you wanted to throw ice water on my hard-on, mention my mother and that's that. Thank God you're a better driver and your hair isn't nearly as big. But you're a damned fine momma."

"Boy oh boy, you're on a roll tonight. Keep that sexy to yourself or I'll have to run them over with your momma's car."

"You know how much I like it when you get all sassy."

She rolled her eyes as the kids barreled into the room, calling out for hugs. She happily gave them and a bunch of kisses goodbye before she headed out. They were going to spend the night with their grandparents, and she was a distant second place to sleeping bags in Grammy's living room and Disney movies with all their cousins.

She was due to pick up Cassie, probably dealing with the same reluctance at leaving her husband behind, in just a few minutes.

Kyle pulled up in front of his brother Marc's house and honked. He knew Liv was driving over to Lily's party with Maggie so at least Marc wouldn't be tangled up in his wife.

For a change.

Each of them had a beautiful wife and wonderful family, but the chemistry between his little brother and his wife was off the charts and the two had a hard time keeping their hands off each other.

Which was probably why Kyle suspected there'd be at least one or two more babies from them. Funny how it was the Chase everyone had thought was the least responsible who'd settled down with a wife and a houseful of kids.

It fit Marc. The ever larger family, the noisy house. He and Liv managed the chaos with humor and a lot of love.

He smiled, thinking of his own three babies. He hadn't just been flattering his way into Maggie's underpants when he'd told her she was a wonderful mother. Given the dreadful example she'd grown up with, Maggie parented like it was easy, or natural, and neither was true.

She was the foundation of their family, and it filled him up to near bursting that he had the life he did. And that his wife was the sexiest thing he'd ever seen.

"Dude, why are you looking like you hit your head on something?" Marc slid into the passenger seat.

"Just thinking about my lovely bride. You ready? I told Shane we'd pick him up at the station. Matt will meet us there too."

"Ready. Liv took the kids over to Mom and Daddy's. She called me after to say their place was a madhouse of tiny Chases and Momma looked like she was in heaven."

"You'd think after getting rid of the four of us they'd be off traveling and enjoying their lives quietly." Kyle snorted as he headed to the police station. "But no, they really do seem to love being grandparents. Which is good because there are times I'm pretty sure the kids like them better than us."

"Hell, I would too."

Shane and Matt waited on the sidewalk as Kyle pulled up.

"Christ it's cold out tonight." Shane shivered as he pulled his seatbelt on.

"I'm sure Cassie would have volunteered to warm you up if you'd asked." Matt elbowed Shane. "Move over."

Shane elbowed him back. "I'm as over as I'm gonna get. Suck it up. As for my wife? I haven't seen her all day, actually. I had an early call, which interrupted a pretty damned good start to the morning." He sighed. "I couldn't even escape for a nice lunch at home it was so busy. Sometimes I think the cold weather makes people act even worse than they do in full summer."

"Unlike you fools, I got some this morning so I'm nice and

relaxed." Matt sat back, Kyle was sure, with a big smile on his face.

There was a muffled *ouch,* most likely from Shane thumping Matt in annoyance.

All was right with the world. Kyle grinned as he drove toward the Tonk.

Chapter Two

Beth knocked on Lily's door and nearly got mowed down by Nathan, William and Joe as they made their way out of the house.

Joe stopped with a smile on his face. One just for her and she gave him one back. "Hey lookit that. It's Joe Harris, the man I love."

"It is indeed. Sorry I missed you this morning."

She'd slept over at his place but he'd had to be awake way earlier and off to work. He'd gotten up so quietly it hadn't even woken her. Even Buck, his—*their*—dog had been quiet and let her sleep.

"You could have woken me up, you know. I'd even have made you breakfast." And jumped his bones.

He gave her a hug, stealing a kiss as her brothers groaned. "Hush up, you two." Joe gave Nathan and William a look before turning back to Beth. "You looked so sweet there, I didn't want to disturb you."

"Also, you were quiet so he probably was in shock."

She looked around Joe to William, Joe's best friend and her older brother. "Ha." Then back to Joe. "You, on the other hand, are totally going to reap the benefits of that compliment later on tonight when we get home."

"Behave yourself now." Joe raised his brow.

"Us? You guys are going to be in a bar, for goodness' sake! We'll be in the back room at the Pumphouse."

"You and your sisters are capable of getting into trouble anytime, anywhere."

She may have snickered. "Says you. Who probably had a chair named after him in the principal's office."

He grinned. "I'll never tell. I've tamed my wild ways. All for you."

"You're totally going to hell for lying." Nathan poked Joe who winced and socked him back.

"Okay, boys, enough with the pokey, punchy. I need him in one piece and I'm sure Lily would also appreciate Nathan not being bruised up. Which he will be if he lets any of those big-haired, mammoth-hootered hoochies anywhere near your table. I'm just saying." She fluttered her lashes.

Joe laughed and kissed her one more time. "I'll do my best to avoid any of those."

"You'd better, or I'm going to let Buck eat SpaghettiOs and then sleep on your side of the bed."

"You're diabolical. He loves that stuff too." He got closer. "You sure you don't want to ditch this stuff and spend some time at home?"

"You're a temptation. But I have penis hats. Penis hats, Joe. Where would I use them if it wasn't for a bachelorette party? I bet you'd be stingy and not let me wear one out to dinner. Heaven knows Nathan is too prissy to let me wear one to the wedding."

"God, I'm glad she's your problem now." William ushered Nathan and Joe down the walk. "He loves you. You love him. Kiss kiss. Now go on and stay out of trouble."

She waved, laughing, and headed into Lily's.

"Hey, ugly, you ready to go eat too much and try to avoid birth stories?"

Lily stood with her brother Chris in the living room. He blushed. "Birth stories?"

"Dude, you don't even want to know. I don't even want to know, but something happens to women when they get around each other and they're mothers. It's like giving birth twists them and they've got PTSD and they have to share the most horrible stuff. Leaking. Bursting. *Tearing.*"

"Gross!"

Laughing, Lily tossed a pillow at Beth's head. "Stop that. You're going to scar him."

"Why should I be alone? Amirite, Christopher? Sharing is loving. You coming with us tonight?"

The look of horror on his face made her laugh anew. "No! I'm spending the night at a friend's house."

There was a honk outside. He went to look and came back, grabbing his bag. "It's Jesse's mom."

"I'll be right back." Lily went out with her brother.

She pulled her phone out and dialed one of her sisters. "You get the cake?"

Anne gave orders in the background and then turned her attention to Beth. "Yes. It's already at the Pumphouse. I'm just waiting for Tate. Looks like Polly has eleven thousand presents for Lily. We invited her, by the way, and Edward assured her he could handle the kids if she wanted to come out. But we're no competition for all these babies. I swear if she could roll around in them like a cat in catnip she would."

Beth laughed because it was true. Polly loved children. Oh sure, people talked about how they loved kids or whatever, but

215

it was a rare breed who loved them as much as Polly Chase did. Poopy diapers, whatever. And she had magic with them. They rarely acted up with her. They seemed to adore her—with a little fear mixed in—like everyone else did.

They'd never get love like that from Beth, Tate and Anne's mother, so it was doubly wonderful that they had Polly in their lives.

"We'll see you over there in a few. I'm at Lily's now, and we'll head over. I know Cassie and Liv are there already. I stopped over on my way here, and the room is set up. I went over the details with them and they're on it."

"I bet you did. I bet you made them go over the plan on a two-minute increment scale."

Busted. "There is nothing wrong with being organized."

"Don't be so touchy, Miss Priss. We'll see you guys in a bit. I'm going to say, up front, that since Tate isn't drinking it's only fair we drink twice as hard."

"So noted." She hung up as Lily came back inside.

"He's doing great, but I feel like if I let up even a little bit he'll backslide."

"I don't think going out to say hello to an adult you're entrusting him to is you being mean. It lets him know you care *and* that you're not going to fall for any old *I'm sleeping at Fred's house* line when he's staying out all night getting girls pregnant or whatever."

"God. Let's change that subject." Lily looked Beth up and down. "That's cute. And conveniently my size."

"Come on, moocher. It's time for your bridal shower."

They took Beth's car over to the Pumphouse and found a spot a block away. It was a Friday night, and Main Street businesses, especially the restaurants, were already filling up.

"I know I'm supposed to have doubts, or cold feet, but I don't." Lily said this quietly as they headed up the sidewalk.

Beth turned, smiling. "You have a big heart and you're smart. It wasn't time all those years ago between you. Not for you or for Nathan. But now? It's perfect. You're strong enough to deal with the stuff that comes with marrying him. Namely all of us. And he's man enough to know what he's got in you, and he knows to grab you and hold you close forever."

"You're a really good best friend, you know that?"

She opened the door and the sound of Petal on a Friday greeted them both. "I do try. Mainly because I love you. But also because I love Nathan and I love seeing him happy."

People called out hellos as they walked through, toward the party room in the back where everyone had already gathered. When they came through the door, there was much hooting and clapping and laughing.

"Whooo! Come on in and sit down." Anne pointed to the chair at the head of the big table that Beth had decorated earlier that afternoon.

Lily saw it and stopped, mouth agape. "A plus to you, Beth Murphy, for this astonishing array of penis and penis-related merchandise."

"We're just getting started. Sit!"

Laughing, Lily sat and then took the penis-festooned pink fedora hat. "You're the guest of honor so you get the best hat." She handed out the rest. "Don't be jealous, there's plenty of penis hats to go around."

She put hers on right as the first round of beer and food came in.

Maggie laughed at the penis straws. "Where did you find all this stuff?"

"I'm sure the FBI is going to be keeping me and my internet searches on file for a while. But there is an unbelievable wealth of penis party favors. This is just about half of what was out there. Some of it I thought might get us arrested. So I refrained because even though we know the sheriff, I'm pretty sure he wouldn't want Cassie to play with us anymore if we got her in trouble."

"I do think all the bridesmaids should wear these blinky penis pins on our dresses for the wedding though." Anne affixed one to her shirt.

Lily nodded. "Sure. It can be our something new."

Fresh giggles broke out, and the server just shook his head, grinning as he left.

"Why are penises evocative of bridal showers anyway? I mean, hello, none of us has one."

"Maybe it's for ladies who are chaste. So they might get spooked when they see one the first time. Get 'em used to what is to come. Not that we're talking Lily. I mean hello."

More laughter.

"We always do it in the pitch dark so I won't get scared." Lily couldn't get through the whole sentence without laughing.

"Damn it, I'm trying to drink some beer but if you keep making me laugh I'm going to choke and then someone will have to give me the Heimlich and forever we'll remember this as *that one time Anne Murphy nearly choked to death at Lily's bridal shower.* Now hold on with the hardy har har long enough for me to get some beer and a nacho or two down, and then the levity may resume."

"I like how she was so dainty just then," Cassie said as she took a drink of her beer.

"Everyone always associates Anne with dainty. It's a curse I bet." Maggie blinked innocently at Anne, who snickered. "I do have so many memories of these nachos."

"Is this a kinky sex thing, Maggie? I heard that about you, but I didn't want to say anything." Tate leaned forward. "Not that it should stop you from telling us if it is."

Maggie shook her head. "No, you pervs! A long time ago I was in here and carrying nachos and Shane bumped into me and spilled them all over me and he was a total dick about it. But it wasn't six months after that that Kyle and I ended up together."

"Us pervs? Girl, you dated one brother before you ended up with the other one. Floozy!" Cassie, who also happened to be Shane's wife, snorted.

"I'm not the only one!" Maggie pointed at Liv. "She did it too."

"You're such a tattletale." Liv just waggled her brows.

Tate, now married to Matt, who Liv dated years before, clapped her hands over her ears. "Lalalalalala."

"Hush you. All fecund and round with the man's baby. Again."

Things had been a little rocky at first between Tate and Liv. Tate had been intimidated by Liv who was ridiculously gorgeous. But after a brief back-and-forth, Liv had just kept pushing herself into Tate's life until she gave in. The two had been good friends ever since, and as Liv absolutely adored Marc and Matt pretty much worshipped Tate, there wasn't anything to worry over.

Lily patted Tate's hand and stole one of her wings while she was at it. "I had a friend in Macon express dismay that someone might date two brothers, and I said, *girl, have you ever lived in a small town?*"

The table dissolved into laughter again.

Beth held up her glass. "The first toast tonight goes to Lily. Who will be marrying our dumbhead brother Nathan in just a few weeks and then it'll be too late, she'll be a Murphy. She keeps Nathan in line and smiling and so sex addled he mainly stays out of my business so thank you, Lily, and welcome to our messed-up family!"

Glasses raised as everyone toasted the woman of the evening.

"Here's to Lily, who knows just how crazy we all are and who stays anyway!"

"And to Lily, who has awesome shoes in my size!"

Barbecued chicken came out right as a few other people arrived. Penny and Dee, two friends who'd moved to Atlanta but always came back for the fun stuff, and Jill with the other two Murphy wives.

"Just in time, I see." Jill, the youngest Murphy sibling, grabbed a glass and the pitcher as she sat. "Sorry, it was a hellish day at work. I have a client who thinks he's god. He's really just a pain in my butt."

"It's all right, there's plenty of food, drink and penis paraphernalia for all." Anne handed down hats and blinky pins. "There are penis sweet tarts too. The purple ones taste like tears and loneliness so avoid those."

Jill curled her lip and held up a purple sugar penis. "If a real penis was purple, it might also taste like tears and loneliness."

Beth nodded. "Especially if it was that small. Still, let's not find out."

Jill raised her brows. "Good to know Joe's wedding tackle isn't tiny and purple."

"I'll give you five dollars to ask him about it." Anne snickered.

Tate clapped. "I'll give you ten to ask William about it. It's fun to watch that vein on his temple throb when he's forced to confront the fact that his baby sister and his best friend are doing dirty sexytimes."

Jill made herself a plate. "The thing I love most about you, Tate, is how you look so sweet on the outside. All maternal with that pretty pale hair and you are just such a troublemaker. I admire that."

"I can guarantee you those boys are not having anywhere near as much fun as we are." Liv sat back in her chair. "Hey, do these dick lollipops have gum in them?"

"I'm not sure where I stand on dick lollipops with stuff in the middle."

"You're all going to ruin our sweet baby Jill." Beth put an arm around her sister.

"Please. Have you met Jill?" Anne waved it away.

"I know, Anne needs to tell us what the hell is going on with Royal."

Anne heaved a sigh and Beth felt bad for her.

"I think it's truly over. We're way better off as friends and I'm not just saying that. He wants marriage. White picket fences and babies. I don't. I don't want that life and I care about him. He should be happy and he can't be with me. And I don't want to feel guilty all the time about not giving him what he needs. I think we're both in love with each other, but it's not deep enough. Not to weather this. I'd never ask him to keep hanging on, waiting around to see if maybe I'll change my mind. He deserves to be in love with someone who wants that as much as he does."

"That's too bad. I like Royal. I like you two together." Tate handed the platter of tacos down to their end of the table.

"I like him too. I've liked him since we were kids. I think we can be better friends. I do know for sure that I can't commit to him like he deserves."

Beth understood it. Anne had a rough time getting past the idea that marriage was what their parents had. It didn't matter that her married siblings didn't have marriages that looked anything like what they'd grown up with. She didn't want to mess up her life, or anyone else's, the way their parents did to one another and to their kids. Some childhood scars ran deep and never healed.

It wasn't like Beth wanted to say Anne'd change her mind. Who knew if Anne ever would, and it was insulting when women told other women they'd change their mind about major life stuff like marriage and kids. She respected each and every one of her siblings and their right to make whatever choices they needed to be happy.

"Now that I've calmed down all the hilarity with my spinster news, how about we open some presents?" Anne winked at Beth, who tipped her chin back at her sister. Anne knew Beth would always have her back, no matter what.

"So it's time for some presents!" Beth stood. "Well, first it's time for cake. Then presents. Anne, can you guys clear off a spot on the table? I'm just going to go find Pete to have him bring the cake in."

Which was easy enough. She wove her way through the crowd and found him near the bar. "Hey, Pete, can we get the cake when you get the chance?"

"You sure can. Everything else all right?"

"Food is excellent. Beer is tasty. I appreciate the help tonight."

"It's always a pleasure to have a bunch of pretty women in here. Not like that's a chore." He winked. As he was nearing eighty, it wasn't like his flirting was serious. "When will we be hosting your bachelorette party?"

She laughed. "I'm enjoying the living-in-sin part right now. We'll get there though."

Pete came around, and they walked back to the kitchen to get the cake from the walk-in.

"How's Joe's daddy?"

Joe's father had been struggling with mental illness for some time, and over the last few months had finally found a medication combo that was working. Rather than respond or act in a way that continued to stigmatize the issue, Beth wanted to treat it like any other health issue. It was, of course, up to Joe's father, and she was careful about what she shared. But when she did talk about it, she did in a very straightforward way. Joe seemed to prefer it and that's what mattered most to her.

"He's better. Working on it."

"You tell him I said hello. My Missy said she ran into Joe's momma the other day at the library, and I've been meaning to ask after him. But it's hard. I don't know what to say."

She nodded. "I understand." Joe's father could be at turns grateful and resentful when people asked after him. But she knew he appreciated that people thought about him, and it really helped his wife, who was trying her damndest to understand his illness and do what was right and best.

Pete looked down at the cake and blushed. "Well lookie here. Who'd have thought they'd make a cake like this?"

She waggled her brows. "There's a novelty cake shop in Riverton."

"Novelty huh?" He laughed as she took the cake from his arms. "I'll have to take a pass on the part where you cut into it." He winced and they headed separate ways.

"I understand. Thanks, Pete."

She came back in and when everyone looked up and saw what she had, snickers and guffaws broke out.

"Oh my lands! Girl, you have pricks on the brain." Lily laughed.

The cake was actually a bunch of small cakes. Little jumping penises. Some had tennis shoes on the balls. Some were floppy. Some had little caps. Sure, she could have gone with something serious, but Lily had a lot of serious trying to keep her brother in line and hoping her mother would come home from sober living in time for the wedding. A little dick humor was just the thing.

And seeing Lily blush and giggle as she blew out all those candles and sliced up all the little dick cakes, Beth was very glad she'd done it.

Chapter Three

"I think I'm going to have to eat an entire packet of Tums after all these wings." Nathan patted his belly.

"Wait until you get in your late thirties. Just looking at something deep fried gives you heartburn."

"Bummer. I'm gonna hate being as old as you, William. Then again, you'll always be older than me. So there's that."

William reached over and socked Nathan's arm. "Asshole."

Their waitress had kept the beer and the food coming as they all hung out, told lies and insulted each other. In other words, a pretty fun night out with his friends.

Joe seemed to find it hilarious that Nathan's ex-fiancé—more like a psycho who announced in the newspaper that they were engaged without talking to Nathan first—kept staring over at their table.

"Steffie can't take her eyes off you." Joe laughed and laughed.

"Quiet or I'll send some beers over to Dolly's table, and then you'll have to deal with my sister. I heard her threaten you about, what did she say..."

"Big-haired, mammoth-hootered skanks I believe was the phrase she used. My romantic, fragile flower."

"I believe she said hoochie instead of skank. My sister does have a way with words." William snorted. "Also, she's scary. Oh sure, she's wise cracking and has a big heart, they all do. But she would take any of those women down if they ever really tried to get in between you."

"I know. It's hot. Not that I'd want her to get into it with anyone. But I can imagine it all I want and if you say anything I'll deny it. Anyway, Jacob and Trey are single. They can run interference."

Jacob, the youngest Murphy brother shook his head and put his hands up. "No thank you. I'm single but I don't have a death wish. I'm not jumping in front of that crazytrain if it barrels over here."

"I might forgive the way Trey put his hands on Beth if he took one for the team." Joe raised a brow, still thinking about the big old slap in the face with the reality that his woman could and would move on if he didn't get his shit straight.

"You should thank me for that. If she'd asked some dude who didn't care about her as much as I do, he might have really made a move."

"He's got a point." Jacob raised a beer.

Joe muttered something but no one got punched so it was all right.

"When are you asking Beth to marry you?"

"You're mean when your crazy ex is staring at you with those googly eyes of hers."

Nathan cracked up. He had a damned good life. Surrounded by his friends and family, celebrating the fact that he would be marrying the love of his life in a few weeks. Growing up in that shitty little trailer, he wasn't always sure he'd make it to the next week, much less end up a schoolteacher and marrying a woman like Lily.

"Hush you. I'm gonna marry the prettiest woman in town, and we're gonna have pretty, dark-haired babies who love their daddy best. My sister may treat your damned dog like a person and act like a loon, but she's a good woman and you'd be lucky to have her as your wife."

Joe nodded. "She's the best. But we're moving at our own pace. There will be a wedding, but we'll get there when we're ready. You think Beth would put up with anything less than exactly what she wanted?"

Everyone laughed at the very idea.

"Exactly. I surely do love that woman and she will be my missus when the time comes. Right now, we're enjoying living in sin and being an aunt and uncle who are able to give y'all's kids back at the end of the day."

"A toast then, to Nathan and Lily." William raised his glass. "You're a lucky guy she's willing to overlook your tragic appearance and marry you. I hope your babies take after her."

"Hear, hear!" Nathan raised his glass as well. "And a toast to the lovely, feisty women of Petal, who make us pancakes, tolerate our bullshit and fill our lives with nice smells, boobs and a warm body to snuggle with in the morning."

More raised glasses. "Hell yes!"

"Hey, where's Royal?" Matt looked around as if he'd just realized their friend wasn't with them.

Joe shrugged. "He and Anne broke off. For real this time. He's spending a week in Los Angeles with his brother."

William sighed. "I think it's for the best. Annie doesn't want to get married. I don't know that she ever will. He wants to settle down. She can't give it to him, and so it's the fairest thing she can do to finally break things off for real. She's too good a person to string him along. They'll be friends, I think. They have been since they were bitty kids. But it's going to take a while for

227

him to truly let go and move on."

"I get it. You can be with someone you like but they're just not the one. There's no need to settle. Liv moved on and found Marc. I found Tate. The right person is out there. I hope they both find that."

"Yeah, me too."

"We need a round of shots, I think." Kyle hailed their server.

Nathan wanted his sister to be happy. As happy as he was. But each of them found happiness on their own terms, and he had every confidence Anne would too.

But that night he was celebrating his own happily ever after with Lily, and all was right with his world. Crazy, googly-eyed ex-whatevers notwithstanding.

"To the right one." Nathan held his shot glass up.

Many shots and pitchers of beer later, Joe looked up to catch sight of Beth, a smile curving her lips, walking in his direction.

He stood and moved to her, pulling her into a hug. "Hello there, darlin'. What are you doing here?"

"We figured you boys might like a ride home. We've got us some designated drivers and stuff. Then we can go home." Her brow rose. "You know, in case there was something you'd like to do there. With me."

"Hell yes."

He turned to make his goodnights but saw pretty much the same situation playing out with their friends kissing up on their women and plans being made to rush off home and get some.

"Before we all head off into the night, I want to thank Beth for organizing my party and for all the penis gear." Lily bowed, holding on to her penis fedora so it wouldn't fall off.

"I'm sure I don't want to know what penis gear is. I'm not going to wear anything weird. Just know that." Joe kissed Beth's ear and she laughed. That's when he noticed the blinking penis pin on her lapel and the plastic penis charms on her bracelet. And the hat.

He sighed, grinning. "You're trouble, Beth Murphy."

"I totally am. You gonna take me to school?"

"Well, everyone, goodnight now." He grabbed her hand as Nathan was thanking everyone for his night out. They waved at the door and headed home to their apartment and their dog and their bed.

Nathan and Lily watched their hasty retreat. "They're next, you know that, right?"

Lily nodded. "Oh yes. She's so in love with him she can barely see straight. And yet, I think this is the steadiest I've ever seen her. She knows what she wants with such total surety."

"Yes, that's a good way to put it. He's been good for her, but I really think she was just exactly what he needed too." He pulled her close. "I know how that feels. There was a time I thought I'd lost the best thing I'd ever had. And now look at me, standing with my arms around my best thing. Who happens to be wearing a hat with tiny penis balloons on it."

"Your sister knows how to decorate a party. You should have seen the cake."

"I'm a little scared, actually."

Lily laughed. "Come on. Chris is gone until tomorrow and we have the house all to ourselves. I think we should take advantage of that."

"You're on."

About the Author

To learn more about Lauren Dane, please visit www.laurendane.com. Send an email to Lauren at laurendane@laurendane.com or find her at Twitter @LaurenDane.

This time, he plans to do it with class. Style.
And more than a little groveling...

Once and Again
© 2011 Lauren Dane
Petal, Georgia, Book 1

Seven years ago, Lily Travis was only too glad to see her hometown of Petal, Georgia, in her rearview mirror. Thanks to her father running off with a twenty-year-old, though, here she is, trying to pick up the pieces. First order of business: meet with her brother's teacher in a quest to pull his grades out of a downward spiral.

Nathan Murphy is pretty much resigned to his bachelor status—until he looks up from his desk to see an all-grown-up Lily walking into his classroom. Of all the women who turned out to be totally wrong for him, she's the only one who felt right. At least until his foolish, immature mistake drove her away.

Lily has to admit that time has been more than kind to gorgeous, sexy Nathan. Except there's no room on her full plate for another complication. Especially with a man who broke her heart once before.

With a little help from his friends, Nathan has a plan to rekindle the flame. It isn't long before they're burning up the sheets. Winning her heart? That's another matter.

Warning: Hot, sexy high school teacher in denim and boots. Strong-willed females abound. Bad words and naughtiness, too. Come on, you know you want to read it.

Available now in ebook and print from Samhain Publishing.

It's all about the story...

Romance

HORROR

Retro ROMANCE

www.samhainpublishing.com